I0640676

Edward G. Browne

Chahar Maqala

Edward G. Browne

Chahar Maqala

ISBN/EAN: 9783337384739

Printed in Europe, USA, Canada, Australia, Japan

Cover: Foto ©Andreas Hilbeck / pixelio.de

More available books at **www.hansebooks.com**

THE

CHAHÁR MAQÁLA

("FOUR DISCOURSES")

OF

NIDHÁMÍ-I-'ARÚDÍ-I-SAMARQANDÍ.

TRANSLATED INTO ENGLISH

BY

EDWARD G. BROWNE, M.A., M.B.,

FELLOW OF PEMBROKE COLLEGE, CAMBRIDGE.

[*Reprinted from the* JOURNAL OF THE ROYAL ASIATIC SOCIETY,
July and October, 1899.]

HERTFORD:
PRINTED BY STEPHEN AUSTIN AND SONS.

1899.

CONTENTS.

THE CHAHÁR MAQÁLA.

In my article on *The Sources of Dawlatsháh*, which appeared in the January number of the Journal, I have already spoken of the excellent work which I now have the pleasure to present in English dress. For my translation I have used the Tihrán lithographed edition of A.H. 1305, which I have carefully collated throughout with the older of the two British Museum MSS. (Or. 3,507, dated A.H. 1017), and, in all doubtful passages, with the second MS. (Or. 2,955, dated A.H. 1274) also. These MSS. are fully described in Rieu's *Persian Supplement*, pp. 244–245 and 265, Nos. 390 and 418. It remains only to say a few words concerning the author and the book.

The *Chahár Maqála* contains, as its name implies, four discourses, each of which treats of a class of men deemed by the author indispensable for the service of kings, to wit, (1) scribes (*dabírán*) or secretaries; (2) poets; (3) astrologers; and (4) physicians. Each discourse begins with certain general considerations on the class in question, which are afterwards illustrated by anecdotes, drawn, in large measure, from the personal reminiscences of the author, who was himself a court-poet and a frequenter of royal assemblies. The total number of these anecdotes, which constitute at once the most entertaining and the most valuable portion of the book, is about forty, an average of ten to each "discourse." So far as I know, only two of them, one concerning Firdawsí and the other about 'Umar Khayyám, have hitherto been cited from this work. Of these the first (translated by Ethé in vol. xlviii of the

Z.D.M.G., pp. 89–94) was taken, not from the *Chahár Maqála* itself, but from Ibn Isfandiyár's *History of Ṭabaristán*, where it is quoted *in extenso*; while the second seems to have been known only in abridged citations, the misunderstanding of which gave rise to the Rose-tree cult of the 'Umar Khayyám Society, referred to at p. 414 of the April number of the Journal.

Of the excellent style of the *Chahár Maqála*, a style at once strong, concise, and pregnant with meaning, though not always easy or simple, I have already spoken at pp. 40, 53, 56–57, and 61–69 of the January number of the Journal, so that there is no occasion to insist upon it further. As, however, my translation will occupy two numbers of the Journal, it may be convenient that I should here give a brief table of its contents.

INTRODUCTORY (*Tihrán ed.*, pp. 1–27).

(1) *Doxology, and Dedication to the Ghúríd Prince Abu'l-Ḥasan 'Alí b. Mas'úd, son of Fakhru'd-Dín Mas'úd, brother of Shamsu'd-Dín Muḥammad, and nephew of "the World-consumer" (Jahán-súz) 'Alá'u'd-Dín Ḥusayn who reigned* A.D. 1149–1170 (pp. 1–6).

(2) *Beginning of the book. The author here gives his full name as Aḥmad b. 'Umar b. 'Alí an-Nidhámí as-Samarqandí, and states that he has been in the service of the House of Ghúr for forty-five years* (pp. 6–7).

(3) *Excursus* i, *on the different grades of Being, and the Creation and Disposition of the World* (pp. 7–11).

(4) *Excursus* ii, *on the Development of the Mineral, Vegetable, and Animal Kingdoms* (pp. 11–14).

(5) *Excursus* iii, *on the Evolution, Faculties, and Senses (internal and external) of Man; the three classes of men; and the Kingly and Prophetic Offices* (pp. 14–26), *including—*

(6) *Anecdote* i, *on the Nasnás, or Wild Man* (pp. 20–21), *and ending with—*

(7) *Plan of work and brief statement of contents* (pp. 26–27).

First Discourse: Secretaries (pp. 27–59).

Nature of the Secretarial Function and Qualifications of the Perfect Scribe (pp. 27–33).[1]

Anecdote ii, *concerning Iskáfí* (pp. 33–36).

Anecdote iii, *on Iskáfí's despatch announcing the defeat of Mákán* (pp. 36–40).

Anecdote iv, *showing that a Secretary of State should not be exposed to domestic worry* (pp. 40–42).

Anecdote v, *concerning the Ṣáḥib Isma'íl ibn 'Abbád* (pp. 42–43).

Anecdote vi, *concerning Aḥmad Ḥasan of Maymand and the Lamghán deputies* (pp. 43–46).

Anecdote vii, *concerning al-Ma'mún's wedding* (pp. 46–51).

Anecdote viii, *concerning al-Mustarshid's oration against the Seljúqs* (pp. 51–53).

Anecdote ix, *concerning the Gúr Khán* (pp. 53–54).

Anecdote x, *concerning the supernatural eloquence of the Qur'án* (pp. 54–55).

Anecdote xi, *concerning Muḥammad b. 'Abdu'lláh, Bughrá Khán's secretary* (pp. 55–59).

Second Discourse: Poets (pp. 59–113).

Nature of the Poetic Art, and Qualifications of the Expert Poet (pp. 59–69), *including—*

Anecdote xii, *concerning Aḥmad b. 'Abdu'lláh of Khujistán* (pp. 59–61), *and—*

List of the eminent poets who have shed lustre on the courts of the various Persian dynasties down to the author's time (pp. 62–64).

Anecdote xiii, *concerning Rúdagí's skill in improvisation* (pp. 69–76).

Anecdote xiv, *concerning Maḥmúd and Ayáz, and 'Unṣurí's improvisation* (pp. 76–79).

Anecdote xv, *concerning Farrukhí's improvisation* (pp. 79–87).

[1] p. 31 is by mistake omitted in the pagination, which, for convenience of reference, I have followed without correction.

THIRD DISCOURSE: ASTROLOGERS (pp. 113–138).

FOURTH DISCOURSE: PHYSICIANS (pp. 138–173).

As regards the author, Niẓámí-i-'Arúḍí of Samarqand, he will best reveal himself by his own numerous allusions to his career and adventures. His present work was written, at least in part, during the lifetime of 'Alá'u'd-Dín Ḥusayn *Jahán-súz* ("the World-consumer"), who died in A.D. 1161, and since he speaks of himself as having been forty-five years in the service of the House of Ghúr, it is evident that he must have been born towards the end of the eleventh century of our era. The chief dates which he gives in the autobiographical portions of his work are as follows. In A.H. 504 (A.D. 1110–1111) he heard traditions concerning Rúdagí at Samarqand (Anecdote xiii). In A.H. 506 (A.D. 1112–1113) he met 'Umar Khayyám at Níshápúr (Anecdote xxvii). In A.H. 509 (A.D. 1115–1116) he was at Herát (Anecdote xvii). In the following year he was at Níshápúr (Anecdote i) and Ṭús (Anecdotes xvi and xx), where he visited Firdawsí's tomb. His position and income were at this time precarious, but, encouraged by the poet Mu'izzí, he succeeded in attracting the king's notice and winning his approval. In A.H. 512 (A.D. 1118–1119) he was again at Níshápúr (Anecdote xxxi), and once more in A.H. 530 (A.D. 1135–1136), when he visited 'Umar Khayyám's grave, and remarked the fulfilment of the prediction uttered by the Astronomer-poet twenty-four years earlier (Anecdote xxvii). In A.H. 547 (A.D. 1152–1153) he was involved in the defeat of the army of Ghúr by Sanjar b. Malikshâh the Seljúq, and was for a while in hiding at Herát (Anecdotes xxx and xli). His life, in short, seems to have been spent chiefly in Khurásán at royal courts, where he had opportunities of meeting many noteworthy persons. Though a poet by profession, he seems to have been equally ready to practise Astrology (Anecdote xxx) and Medicine (Anecdote xli). Of his personal character, as of his ability, his work produces, on the whole, a very favourable impression, and the book itself I should be disposed to describe as one of the most interesting, the most instructive, the most charming, and the best written Persian prose works which it has been my fortune to come across. Of this, however, the reader shall judge for himself.

Notices of the writer occur in 'Awfí's *Lubábu'l-Albáb* (ch. x, § 2, Poets of Transoxania), from which we learn nothing about his personality save that he bore the *laqab* of Najmu'd-Dín; Dawlatsháh's *Tadhkira* (Ṭabaqa i, No. 13, pp. 60–61 of my forthcoming edition), where laudatory mention is made of the *Chahár Maqála*; Hájí Khalífa (No. 4,348, s.v. چهار مقاله), who calls him *Nidhámu'd-Dín* (instead of *Najmu'd-Dín*), which is probably correct; the

Majma'u'l-Fuṣaḥá of that most accomplished of recent Persian writers, Riḍá-qulí Khán (vol. i, p. ٦٣٥), who places him higher as a prose-writer than as a poet; and, no doubt, other biographical works. But, leaving these aside, let us now allow the author to speak for himself, only promising that, where reference is made to various readings, the older MS. (Or. 3,507) is denoted by A, the other MS. (Or. 2,955) by B, and the Tihrán lithographed edition by L.

THE FOUR DISCOURSES (CHAHÁR MAQÁLA) OF NIDHÁMÍ-I-'ARÚḌÍ-I-SAMARQANDÍ.

In the Name of God, the Merciful, the Clement.

Praise and thanks and glory to that King who, by[1] the instrumentality of the Cherubim and Angels of the Spirit World, brought into being the World of Return and Restoration, and, by means thereof, created and adorned the World of Becoming and Decay, maintaining it by the Command and Prohibition of the Prophets and Saints, and restraining it by the swords and pens of Kings and Ministers. And blessings upon the Lord of both worlds, who was the most perfect of the Prophets, and invocations of grace upon his Companions and those of his Household, who were the most excellent of Saints and Vicars. And honour to the King of this time, that learned, just, divinely-favoured, victorious, and heaven-aided monarch, *Husámu'd-Dawla wa'd-Dín*, Helper of Islám and the Muslims, Exterminator of the infidels and polytheists, Subduer of the heretical and the froward, Supporter of hosts in the worlds, Pride of Kings and Emperors, Succourer of mankind, Protector of these days, Fore-arm of the Caliphate, Beauty of the Faith and Glory of the Nation, Order of the Arabs and the Persians, noblest of mankind, *Shamsu'l-Ma'álí*,

[1] L. has بلا توسط, "without the intervention."

Maliku'l-Umará, Abu'l-Ḥasan 'Alí b. Mas'úd,[1] Help of the Prince of Believers, may his life be filled with success, may the greater part of the world be assigned to his name, and may the ordering of the affairs of Adam's seed be directed by his care! For to-day he is the most excellent of the kings of the age in nobility, pedigree, doughty deeds, judgement, statesmanship, justice, equity, valour, and generosity, as well as in the adorning of his territory, the embellishment of his realms, the maintenance of his friends, the subjugation of his foes, the raising of armies, the safeguarding of the people, the securing of the roads, and the tranquilizing of the realms,[2] and also in that upright judgement, clear understanding, strong resolve, and firm determination, by the excellence of which the concatenation of the House of Shansab[3] is held together and maintained in order, and by the perfection of which the strong arm of that Dynasty is strengthened and braced. May God Almighty give him full portion, together with the other kings of that line, of dominion and domain, and throne and fortune, by His Favour and His Grace!

But to proceed. It is an old custom and ancient practice, which custom is maintained and observed, that the Author, in the introduction to his discourse and preface of his book, should commemorate somewhat of his patron's praise, and record some prayer on behalf of the object of his eulogy. But I, a loyal servant, instead of praise and prayer for this prince, will make mention in this book of those favours ordained and vouchsafed by God Almighty to this King of kingly parentage, that, these being submitted to his world-illuminating judgement, he may betake himself to the expression of his thanks for them. For in

[1] This Prince belonged to the Bámiyán line of the Ghúrid Dynasty, was the son of Fakhru'd-Dín Mas'úd, and brother of Shamsu'd-Dín Muḥammad, and flourished in the latter part of the sixth century of the *hijra*.

[2] L. has از مهالک, "from perils," instead of ممالک.

[3] See *Ṭabaqát-i-Náṣiri* (ed. Nassau Lees), p. 101 et seqq. The correct reading is found only in A. B. has انسانیت, L. آل شیب.

the uncreated Scripture and unmade Word, God says, "*Verily if ye be thankful, We will give unto you increase*"[1]; for the gratitude of the servant is an alchemy for the favours of the Munificent Lord. Briefly, then, it behoves this great King and puissant Prince to know that to-day, upon the whole of this globe of dust, and within the circle of this green firmament,[2] there is no king in more ample circumstances than this monarch, nor any potentate enjoying more abundant good than this sovereign. He hath the gift of youth and the blessing of constant health; his father and mother are alive; congenial brothers are on his right hand and on his left. And what father is like his sire, the mighty, divinely-strengthened, ever-victorious, heaven-aided *Fakhru'd-Dawla wa'd-Dín*,[3] Prince of the realms of Írán, King of the Mountains (may God prolong his continuance and continue to the heights his exaltation!), who is the most puissant of the monarchs of the age, and the most excellent of the princes of the time in judgement, statecraft, knowledge, chivalry, swordsmanship, strength of arm, treasure, and muniment! Supported by ten[4] thousand men bearing spears and handling reins, he hath made himself a shield before his sons, so that no disturbing blast of the zephyr may so much as blow on one of their servants. Under his high protection and unassailable precaution (may God increase their degree!), prayers, of which each clause is breathed upwards at full morning-tide to the Court of God, co-operate with a far-trailing host and wheeling army. What a brother, too, like the royal Prince *Shamsu'd-Dawla wa'd-Dín*, Light of Islám and the Muslims (may his victories be rendered glorious!), who reaches the extreme limit of endeavour in the service of this my master (whose exaltation may God perpetuate!). Praise be to God that this my master omits naught either

[1] Qur'án, xiv, 7.

[2] A. has چتر, "umbrella," for چرخ, "firmament."

[3] Fakhru'd-Dín Mas'úd b. 'Izzu'd-Dín Ḥasan, A.H. 550 (A.D. 1155).

[4] L. om. "ten."

in reward or retribution![1] And a favour yet greater is this, that the All-Perfect Benefactor and Unchanging Giver hath bestowed on him an uncle like the Lord of the World and Sovereign of the East, *'Alá'u'd-Dunyá wa'd-Dín* Abú 'Alí al-Ḥusayn b. al-Ḥusayn,[2] *Ikhtiyáru Amíri'l-Mú'minín* (may God prolong his life[3] and cause his kingdom to endure!), who, with fifty thousand mail-clad men, strenuous in endeavour, obliterated the hosts of the world, and set in a corner all the kings of the age. May God (blessed and exalted is He!) long vouchsafe all to one another, and give all long enjoyment of one another's company, and fill the world with light by their achievements, by His Favour, and Bounty, and Grace!

Beginning of the Book.

Your loyal servant and faithful retainer Aḥmad b. 'Umar[4] b. 'Alí an-Nidhámí al-'Arúḍí as-Samarqandí, who for forty-five years hath been devoted to the service of this House and inscribed in the register of the vassals of this Dynasty, desireth to render a service to the Supreme Imperial Court (may God exalt it!), and to set forth, according to the canons of Philosophy, duly adorned with decisive proofs, trenchant arguments and sound counsel, what kingship truly is, who is truly king, whence is derived this honourable office, to whom rightly appertaineth this favour, and in what manner one ought to show one's gratitude for, and after what fashion accept, this privilege, so as to be second to the Lord of the children of men and third to the All-Provider of the Universe; for in the

[1] A. adds: بلکه جهان روشن بروی او همی بیند و عمر شیرین بجمال او همی گدارد.

[2] 'Alá'u'd-Dín Ḥusayn, called *Jahan-súz*, "the World-consumer," A.H. 544–556.

[3] L. for عمره has عزّه, "his glory."

[4] L. om. [بن عمر]

Incontrovertible Scripture and Eternal Word God hath co-ordinated on one thread the pearls represented by these three exalted titles: "*Obey God,*" saith He, "*and obey His Apostle, and such as possess authority amongst yourselves.*"[1]

Now in the grades of existences and the ranks of the intelligibles, apart from the prophetic function, which is the supreme limit of man's degree, there is no rank higher than sovereignty, which is naught else but a Divine gift. God, glorious is His Name, hath accorded this position to the King of the age, and bestowed on him this degree, so that he may walk after the way of former kings and maintain the people after the manner of bygone ages.

Excursus I.

The August Discernment (may God exalt it!) must know that every being which inhabits the Universe falls necessarily into one of two categories. Either it is a being which is self-existent, and is called '*the Necessarily Existent,*' which is God Almighty, great is His Glory, who existeth by virtue of Himself, and who, therefore, hath existed for ever, since He dependeth not on aught else; and who was always, since He subsisteth by Himself, not by another. But that existence whose being is through another is called '*Contingent Being,*' and this is such as we are, since our being is from the seed, and the seed is from the blood, and the blood is from food, and food is from the sun, the earth, the water and the air, which in turn are from something else; and all these are such as yesterday were not, and to-morrow will not be. Now when reflection is carried to the uttermost, it appeareth that this Causal Nexus reacheth upwards to a Cause which deriveth not its being from another, but existeth by itself; and that the Creator is all, and from Him all deriveth its existence and subsistence. And when this matter is somewhat pondered, it will become clear that

[1] Qur'án, iv, 62.

Phenomena consist of Being tinctured with Not-being, while He IS by a continuity which reaches from Eternity Past to Eternity to come. And since the essence of Phenomena is of Not-being, they must inevitably return again to nothing; and again, as touching the basis of the human race,[1] it is said, "*Everything shall return unto its Origin,*" more especially in this world of Becoming and Decay. Therefore we, who are contingent in our being, have our origin in Not-being; while He, who existeth necessarily, is the Essence of Being, even as He (glorious is His state) saith in the Perspicuous Word and Firm Support, "*All things perish save His Countenance.*"[2]

Now you must know that this world lies in the hollow of the Heaven of the Moon[3] and within the circle of this first sphere, and is called "the World of Becoming and Decay." And you must thus conceive it, that within the concavity of the Heaven of the Moon lies the Orb of Fire, round about which extends the Heaven of the Moon; and that within the Heaven of Fire is the Air, surrounded by the Fire, and within the Air is the Water, surrounded by the Air, while within the Water is the earth, with the Water round about it. And in the midst of the earth is an imaginary point, from which all straight lines drawn to the Heaven of the Moon are equal; and when we speak of "down," we mean this point and what lies nearest to it; and when we speak of "up," we mean the sphere of the remotest heaven, together with what lies nearest to it, this being a heaven[4] above the Zodiacal Heaven, having nought beyond it, for with it the material world terminates, or comes to an end.

[1] I here follow L., which has: و نیز در بنیان زمرهٔ انسان گفته اند.
A. has نبیّان, "the Prophets of the human race have said."

[2] Qur'án, xxviii, 88.

[3] This is the lowest or innermost of the nine celestial spheres which environ the earth. Concerning the Muslim Cosmogony, see Dieterici's *Makrokosmos*, p. 178 et seqq.

[4] This outermost, or ninth, celestial sphere is the *Primum mobile* of the Ptolemaic system, the *Falaku'l-Atlas* or *Falaku'l-Aflák* of the Muslim philosophers.

Now when God Almighty, by His effective Wisdom, desired to produce in this world minerals, plants, animals, and men, He created the stars, and in particular the sun and moon, whereon he made the growth and decay of these *to* depend. And the special property of the sun is this, that by its reflection it warms all things when it stands over against them, and supplies them through a medium with heat, and draws them up—that is, attracts them. So, by its juxtaposition, it warmed the water; and by means of the warmth, attracted it; until, in a long while, it laid bare one quarter or more of the earth's surface, by reason of the much vapour which ascended and rose up therefrom. Now the nature of the water is this, that it can become stone, as it is well known to do in certain places, as may be actually witnessed.[1] So mountains were produced from the water and the shining of the sun; and hereby the earth became somewhat raised from what it was, while the water sank and dried up, according to that fashion which is witnessed. This portion, therefore, is called '*the Uncovered Quarter*,' for the reason above stated; and it is also called '*the Inhabited Quarter*,' because animals dwell therein.

EXCURSUS II.

When the influences of these stars had acted on the whole of[2] these elements, they were reflected back from the midst of the earth and water, from that imaginary point [mentioned above], by the aid of the fire and wind, and the phenomena of the inorganic world were produced, such as mountains and mines, clouds, lightning, thunder, thunderbolts, shooting stars, comets, meteors, ... ,[3] halos, conflagrations, earthquakes, and all manner of

[1] The author alludes either to petrifaction and the formation of stalactites, or to ice.

[2] A., B., در اقطار, "on [all] parts." L. has و قسط, which seems to me to be nonsense.

[3] A., B., L. add وعصى, a word of which I have been unable to ascertain the meaning.

fountains, as has been fully explained in works treating of the effects of the celestial bodies, but for the explanation and discussion of which there is no room in this brief manual. But when time began, and the cycles of heaven became continuous, and the composition of this lower world became matured, and the time was come for the fertilization of that interspace which lay between the water and the air, the vegetable world was manifested. Then God, blessed and exalted is He, created for that substance whereby the plants were made manifest four subservient forces and three faculties. Of these four subservient forces, one was that which kept drawing to it whatever was suitable for its purpose, and this is called 'Attraction' (*Jádhiba*). Another keeps what the first may have attracted, and this is called 'Fixation' (*Másika*). The third is that which assimilates what has been attracted, and transmutes it from its former state until it becomes like unto itself, and this is called 'Assimilation' (*Háḍima*). The fourth is that which rejects what is not appropriate, and is called 'Excretion' (*Dáfi'a*). And of the three faculties, one is that which increaseth it by diffusing throughout it nutritious matters with a suitable and equal diffusion. The second is that which accompanies this nutriment until it reaches the extremities. The third is that which, when the organism has attained perfection and begins to tend towards defect, appears and produces germs, in order that, if destruction overtake the parent in this world, these may become its substitute and representative, so that the order of the world may be guarded from detriment, and the species may not cease. This is called the 'Reproductive Faculty' (*Quwwat-i-Muwallida*).

So this kingdom rose superior to the mineral and vegetable kingdoms in these several ways which have been mentioned; and the far-reaching Wisdom of the Creator so ordained, that those kingdoms should be connected successively and continuously, so that in the mineral kingdom the first thing which attained completeness and underwent the process of evolution became higher in organization until it grew to coral (*marján*, i.e. *bussad*), which is the ultimate term of the mineral world,[1] until it was connected with the first stage of plant life. And the first thing in the vegetable kingdom is the thorn, and the last the date-palm, which has been assimilated to the animal kingdom, since it needs the male to fertilize it so that it may bear fruit;[2] while another [member of this kingdom] flees from its foe, for the vine flees from the *'ashaqa*,[3] a plant which, when it twists round the vine, causes it to shrivel up. In the vegetable kingdom, therefore, there is nothing higher than the date-palm and the vine, inasmuch as they are connected with the superior kingdom, and have outstepped the limits of their own world, and have evolved themselves in a higher direction.

Excursus III.

Now when this kingdom had attained perfection, and the influence of the 'Fathers' of the upper world had worked on the 'Mothers'[4] below, and these had assumed a finer temper, and the interspace between the air and the fire became involved, and a finer offspring resulted, the manifestation of the animal world took place. This took to itself the faculties possessed by the vegetable kingdom, and added thereunto two others, one the faculty of discovery, which is called the 'Perceptive Faculty' (*Mudrika*), whereby the animal discerns things; the second the power of voluntary movement, by the help of which the animal moves automatically, approaching that which is agreeable to it and retreating from that which is offensive to it; and this is called the 'Motor Faculty' (*Muḥarrika*).

Now the *Perceptive Faculty* is subdivided into ten branches, five of which are called the *External Senses* and five the *Internal Senses*. The former are *Touch*, *Taste*, *Hearing*, *Sight*,

[1] The Pearl, however, seems generally to be placed higher. See Dieterici's *Mikrokosmos*, p. 11.
[2] See Dieterici's *Mikrokosmos*, p. 26.
[3] A species of *Dolichos*. See Lane's Arabic Lexicon, s.v.
[4] By the 'Seven Fathers above' and the 'Four Mothers below' the seven planets and the four elements are intended.

and *Smell*. Now *Touch* is a sense distributed throughout the flesh and skin of the animal, so that the nerves perceive and discern anything which touches it, such as dryness and moisture, heat and cold, roughness and smoothness, harshness and softness. *Taste* is a sense located in that nerve which is distributed over the surface of the tongue, which apprehends tastes and dissolved flavours from those bodies which come in contact with it; and it is this sense which discriminates between sweet and bitter, sharp and sour, and the like of these. *Hearing* is a sense located in the nerve which is distributed about the auditory meatus, so that it detects any sound which is discharged against it by undulations of the air compressed between two impinging bodies, that is to say, two bodies brought into contact with one another, by the impact of which the air is thrown into waves and becomes the cause of sound, inasmuch as it acts upon the air which is stationary in the auditory meatus, comes into contact with it, reaches this nerve, and gives rise to the sensation of hearing. *Sight* is a faculty located in two nerve-bulbs, which discerns images projected on the crystalline humour, whether of figures or solid bodies, variously coloured by the medium of a translucent substance which subsists between it and the surfaces of reflecting bodies. *Smell* is a faculty located in a protuberance situated in the fore part of the brain and resembling the nipple of the female breast, which apprehends what the air inhaled brings to it of odours mingled with the vapours wafted by air-currents, or what is impressed upon it by diffusion from the odorific body.

The Five Internal Senses.[1] Now as to the Internal Senses, some are such as perceive sense-impressions, while others are such as apprehend ideas. The first is the 'Composite Sense' (*Ḥiss-i-mushtarika*), which is a faculty located in the anterior ventricles of the brain, and receptive into itself of any image apprehended by the external senses, or impressed upon them for communication to it, such

[1] See my *Year amongst the Persians*, pp. 144, 145.

perception being apprehended only when received by it. The second is the Imagination (*Khayál*), a faculty located in the posterior ventricles of the second convolution of the brain, which preserves what the *Composite Sense* has apprehended from the external senses, so that this remains in it after the subsidence of the sense-impressions. The third is the 'Imaginative Faculty' (*Mutakhayyila*), thus called when animals are under discussion, but, in the case of the human soul, named the 'Cogitative Faculty' (*Mutafakkira*). This is a faculty located in the middle ventricle of the brain, whose function it is to co-ordinate with one another, and to preserve, those particular percepts which are stored in the *Imagination*, and to keep them distinct from one another by the control of thought. The fourth is the 'Apprehensive Faculty' (*Wáhima*), which is a faculty located in the extremity of the middle ventricle of the brain. Its function is to discover the supra-sensual ideas existing in particular percepts. By it the kid distinguishes between its dam and a wolf, and the child between a piece of rope and a serpent. The fifth is the 'Retentive Faculty' (*Háfidha*), also called the 'Memory' (*Dhákira*), which is a faculty located in the posterior ventricle of the brain. It preserves those supra-sensual ideas discovered by the *Apprehension*; between which and itself the same relation subsists as between the *Imagination* and the *Composite Sense*, though the latter preserves forms and the former ideas.

Now all these are the servants of the *Animal Soul*, a substance having its well-spring in the heart, which, when it acts in the heart, is called the *Animal Spirit*, but when in the brain, the *Psychic Spirit*, and when in the liver, the *Natural Spirit*. It is a subtle vapour which rises from the blood, diffuses itself to the remotest arteries, and resembles the sun in luminosity. Every animal which possesses these Perceptive and Motor faculties, and these ten subordinate faculties derived therefrom, is called a perfect animal; but if any faculty is lacking in it, defective. Thus the snake has no ears, the ant no eyes, and these two are called deaf and blind; but none is more defective than the maggot, which is a red worm found in the mud of streams,[1] called therefore *gil-khwára* ('mud-eater'), but in Transoxania *Za'ák-kirma* (?).[2] This is the lowest animal, while the highest is the satyr (*nasnás*),[3] a creature inhabiting the plains of Turkistán, of erect carriage, of vertical stature, with wide flat nails. It cherishes a great affection for men; wherever it sees them, it halts on their path and examines them attentively; and when it finds a solitary man, it carries him off; nay, it is even said that it will conceive from him. This, after mankind, is the highest of animals, inasmuch as in several respects it resembles man; first, in its erect stature; secondly, in the breadth of its nails and in the hair of its head.

Anecdote i.

I heard as follows from Abú Riḍá b. 'Abdu's-Salám of Níshápúr, in the Great Mosque at Níshápúr, in the year A.H. 510 (=A.D. 1116–1117):—"We were travelling towards Tamgháj,[4] and in our caravan were several thousand camels. One day, when we were marching in the midday heat, we saw on a hillock a woman, bare-headed, extremely beautiful in form, with a figure like a cypress, a face like the moon, and long hair, standing and looking at us. Although I spoke to her, she made no reply; and when I approached her, she fled, running so swiftly in her flight that no horse could overtake her. Our guides,[5] who were

[1] Cf. Dieterici's *Mikrokosmos*, p. 43.

[2] A. reads رعاك كرمه, B. زعاك كرمه, L. زعاك گربه.

[3] The term *nasnás* either denotes a real animal or a fabulous monster. In the first sense it is used of various kinds of monkeys, e.g. the orang-outang and marmoset; in the latter it is equivalent to the *Shiqq* or Half-man (which resembles a man cut in two vertically) of the Arabs, and the *Dív-mardum* of the Persians. See Qazwíní's *'Ajá'ibu'l-Makhlúqát*, p. 449; and my *Year amongst the Persians*, pp. 165, 267.

[4] See Qazwíní's *Áthárú'l-Bilád*, p. 275.

[5] The meaning of this word is conjectural. The sentence runs in A: وکِری کشان ما ترکان بودند. . D. has وکرای کشان, otherwise the same as A. In L. the sentence runs: 'وکوی کشان تا برکان بودند.

Turks, said that this was a wild man, such as they call *nasnâs.*"

Now you must know that it is nobler than other animals in those three respects which have been mentioned.

So when, by lapse of long ages and time, organization waxes more delicate, the moment comes for that interaction which takes place between the elements and the heavens, and man comes into being, bringing with him all that existed in the mineral, vegetable, and animal kingdoms, to which is added the capacity for intellectual concepts. So he becomes king over all, and brings all things under his control. For from the mineral world he made jewels, gold and silver his embellishment and adornment, while from iron, tin, copper, and lead he fashioned utensils for his use. From the vegetable kingdom also he made his food and raiment and carpets; and from the animal world he provided himself with steeds and beasts of burden. Moreover, from all three kingdoms he chose out medicaments wherewith to heal himself. Whence did there accrue to him all this superiority? By this, that he knew himself, and, by means of intellectual concepts, knew God. "*He who knoweth himself, knoweth his Lord.*"

So this kingdom [of man] became divided into three classes. The first is that class which is proximate to the Animal Kingdom, such as the wild men of the waste and the mountain, whose intelligence doth not more than suffice to secure their own livelihood, seek their own advantage, and ward off what is to their detriment. The second class compriseth the inhabitants of towns and cities, who possess civilization, mutually assist one another, and discover crafts and arts; but whose scientific attainments are limited to the organizing of such association as subsists between them, to the end that the different classes[1] may continue to exist. The third class comprises such as are independent of these things, whose occupation, by night and by day, in secret and in public, is to reflect, "Who

[1] Or perhaps "races." The word is ازواج.

are we; for what reason did we come into existence, and who hath brought us into being?" In other words they hold debate concerning the real essences of things, reflect on their coming, and anxiously consider their departure, saying, "How have we come? Whither do we go?"

This class, again, is subdivided into two sorts; first, those who reach the essence of this object by means of masters, by laborious toil and absorption, and by reading and writing; and such are called *philosophers*. But there is yet another sort who, without master or book, reach the extreme limit of this problem, and these are called *prophets*.

Now, the peculiar virtues of the Prophet are three: first, that, without instruction, he knows all knowledges; secondly, that he gives information concerning yesterday and to-morrow otherwise than by analogical reasoning; and thirdly, that his soul hath such power that from whatever body he will he taketh the form and produceth another form, which thing none can do save such as are conformed to the Angelic World. Therefore in the Human World none is above him, and his command is effective for the well-being of the world; for whatever they have, he has, while possessing also an additional qualification which they have not, that is to say, communion with the Angelic World. This additional qualification is in brief termed the *Prophetic Function*, and is in detail such as we have explained.

Now, so long as such a man lives, he points out to his people what things conduce to well-being in both worlds, by the Command of God, glorious is His Name, communicated to him by means of the Angels. But when, by natural dissolution, he turns his face towards the other world, he leaves behind him a Code derived from the indications of God Almighty and his own sayings. And assuredly he requires to set as his substitute, and to maintain his Law and Practice, a vicegerent, who must needs be the most excellent of mankind and the most perfect product of his age, in order that he may revive this Law and carry out this Practice; and such an one is called an *Imám*. This Imám can cope with the disasters of the East and the West, the North and the South, in such wise that the effects of his care extend alike to the most remote and the nearest, while his command and prohibition reach alike the intelligent and the ignorant. But he must needs have vicars to act for him in distant parts of the world, and not every one of these will have such power that all mankind shall be compelled to admit it. Hence there must be a leader, an administrator, a compeller, which administrator and compeller is called a *Monarch*, that is to say, a *King*; and his vicarious function *Sovereignty*. The King, therefore, is the lieutenant of the Imám, the Imám of the Prophet, and the Prophet of God (mighty and glorious is He!).

Well has it been said on this subject:

چنان دان که شاهی و پیغمبری ' دو گوهر بود در یک انگشتری '

"*Then know that the functions of Prophet and King*
Are set side by side like two stones in one ring."

Know, therefore, that the Regal and Prophetic offices are as two jewels in one ring, for the Prince of the sons of men himself hath said "*State and Church are twins*," since in form and essence neither differs, either as regards increase or defect, from the other. So, by virtue of this decree, no burden, after the Prophetic office, is weightier than Sovereignty, nor any function more laborious than that of governing. Hence a king needs round about him, as men on whose counsel, judgement, and deliberations depend the loosing and binding of the world, and the well-being and ill-being of the servants of God Almighty, such as are in every case the most excellent and most perfect of their time.

Now of the special ministers of Kings are the Secretary, the Poet, the Astrologer, and the Physician, and these can in no wise be dispensed with. For the maintenance of the administration is by the Secretary; the perpetuation of immortal renown by the Poet; the ordering of affairs by the Astrologer; and the health of the body by the Physician.

Those four arduous functions and noble arts are amongst the branches of the Science of Philosophy; the functions of the Scribe and the Poet being branches of the Science of Logic; that of the Astrologer, one of the principal subdivisions of Mathematics; while the Physician's Art is amongst the branches of Natural Science. This book, therefore, comprises *Four Discourses*, to wit:—

First Discourse, on the essence of the Secretarial Art, and the nature of the Secretary.

Second Discourse, on the essence of the Poetic Art, and what it behoves the Poet to be.

Third Discourse, on the essence of the Science of Astrology, and the distinguishing signs of the Astrologer.

Fourth Discourse, on the essence of the Science of Medicine, and the function and nature of the Physician.

In all these divisions of Philosophy, then, that will be advanced which is appropriate to this book; and thereafter ten pleasing anecdotes, of the choicest connected with that subject and the rarest germane to that topic, of what hath befallen persons of the class under discussion, will be added, in order that it may become plainly known to the King that the Secretarial Office is not a trivial matter; that the Poetic Calling is no mean occupation; that Astrology is a necessary Science; that Medicine is indispensable; and that the wise King cannot do without these four persons—the Scribe, the Poet, the Astrologer, and the Physician.

First Discourse.

On the Essence of the Secretarial Function and the Nature of the Perfect Scribe.

The Secretarial Function is an art comprising reasoned modes of address and communication, and teaching the forms of address employed amongst men in correspondence, consultation, contention, eulogy, condemnation, diplomacy, provocation, and conciliation, as well as in magnifying matters or minimizing them; contriving means of excuse or censure; imposing covenants; recording antecedents; and displaying, in every case, orderly arrangement, so that all may be enunciated primarily and finally.[1]

Hence the Secretary must be of gentle birth, of refined honour, of penetrating discernment, of profound reflection, and of firm judgement; and the amplest portion and fullest share of the methods and attainments of this art must be his. Neither must he be remote from, or unacquainted with, logical judgements; and he must know the ranks of his contemporaries, and be familiar with the dignities of the leading men of his time. Moreover, he should not be absorbed in the wealth and perishable goods of this world; nor concern himself with the approval or condemnation of prejudiced persons and tattlers, or pay any heed to them; and he should, when exercising his secretarial functions, guard the honour of his master from degrading situations and dangerous practices. And in the course of his letter, while pursuing his duties of correspondence, he should not quarrel with eminent and powerful personages; and, even though enmity subsist between his master and the person whom he is addressing, he should restrain his pen, and not attack him, save in the case of one who may have overstepped his own proper limit, or advanced his foot beyond the circle of respect, for they say: *"One for one,[2] and he who begins is most in the wrong."*

And in his forms of address he should observe moderation, writing to each person that which befits his position, whereunto his kingdom, domain, army, and treasure are a guide; save in the case of one who may himself have fallen short in this matter, or made display of undue pride, or neglected some point of courtesy, or manifested an arrogance which reason cannot regard otherwise than as misplaced in such

[1] i.e. "once and for all," with such clearness as to leave no ambiguity, or ground for future dispute.

[2] واحدٌ بواحدٍ و البادی اظلم, i.e., "Tit for tat, and the aggressor is most to blame."

correspondence, and unsuitable in epistolary communications. In such cases it is permitted and allowed to the Scribe to take up his pen, set his best foot forward, and in this pass go to the extreme limit and utmost bound, for they say: "*Haughtiness towards the haughty is a good work.*"[1] But in no case must he suffer any dust from the atmosphere of conflict in this arena of correspondence to alight on the skirt of his master's honour; and in the setting forth of his message he must adopt that method which the orators of the Arabs have thus described: "*The best speech is that which is brief and significant, and not wearisome.*"[2] For if the ideas accord not with the words, the discussion will be protracted, and the Scribe will be stigmatized as prolix, and "*He who is prolix is a babbler.*"[3]

Now the words of the Scribe will not attain to this elevation until he becomes familiar with every science, obtains some hint from every master, hears some aphorism from every philosopher, and borrows some elegance from every man of letters. Therefore he must accustom himself to peruse the Scripture of the Lord of Glory, the Traditions of Muḥammad the Chosen One (on whom, and on whose family, be God's blessing and peace), the Memoirs of the Companions, the proverbial sayings of the Arabs, and the wise words of the Persians; and to read the books of the ancients, and to study the writings of their successors, such as the *Correspondence* of the Ṣáḥib Isma'íl ibn 'Abbád[4] and Ṣábí; the *Qábús-náma*[5]; the compositions of Ḥamádí, Laqání, and Ibn Qudáma[6]; the *Gests* of Badí'u'z-Zamán

[1] التكبّر مع المتكبّر صدقة.

[2] خير الكلام ما قلّ ودلّ ولم يُمَلّ.

[3] المكثار مهذار.

[4] See the *Yatímatu'd-Dahr* (ed. Damascus), vol. iii, pp. 31–112; De Slane's *Ibn Khallikán*, vol. i, pp. 212–217. L. omits "and Ṣábí."

[5] Composed by Kayká'ús b. Iskandar b. Qábús b. Washmgír in A.H. 475 (A.D. 1082–3). See Pertsch's *Cat. of Berlin Persian MSS.*, pp. 302–3.

[6] See Von Kremer's *Culturgesch.*, i, pp. 269, 270.

al-Hamadání,[1] al-Ḥaríri,[1] and al-Ḥamídí[2]; the *Rescripts* of al-Bal'amí,[3] Aḥmad-i-Ḥasan,[4] and Abú Naṣr Kundurí[5]; the *Letters* of Muḥammad 'Abd, 'Abdu'l-Ḥamíd, and the Sayyidu'r-Ru'asá; the *Séances* of Muḥammad-i-Manṣúr,[6] Ibn 'Abbádí,[7] and Ibnu'n-Nassába, the descendant of 'Alí; and, of the poetical works of the Arabs, the *Díwáns* of Mutanabbí,[8] Abíwardí,[9] and Ghazzí[10]; and, amongst the Persian poets, the poems of Ḥakím Rúdagí,[11] the Epic of Firdawsí,[12] and the panegyrics of 'Unṣurí[13]; since each one of those works which we have enumerated was, after its kind, the incomparable and unique product of its time; and every scribe who hath these books, and stimulates his mind, polishes his wit, and enkindles his fancy by their perusal, will ever raise the level of his diction, whereby a scribe becomes famous.

Now if he be well acquainted with the Qur'án, with one verse therefrom he may discharge his obligation to a whole realm, as did Iskáfí.[14]

[1] See Von Kremer's *Culturgesch.*, ii, pp. 470–476; Brockelmann's *Gesch. d. Arab. Litt.*, pp. 93–94 and 276–278.

[2] See Rieu's *Persian Catalogue*, vol. ii, pp. 747–8, where a very fine old MS. of the *Maqámát-i-Ḥamídí*, written in the thirteenth century of our era, is described.

[3] Abú 'Alí Muḥammad al-Bal'amí (d. A.H. 386).

[4] The Ghaznavid Minister, Aḥmad b. Ḥasan of Maymand (d. A.H. 424), is probably meant.

[5] See De Slane's *Ibn Khallikán*, vol. iii, pp. 290–295.

[6] Probably Muḥammad b. Manṣúr al-Ḥaddád. See *H. Kh.*, No. 1,720.

[7] Abú 'Áṣim Muḥammad b. Aḥmad al-'Abbádí (see Rieu's *Arabic Suppl.*, p. 755), who died A.H. 458, is probably intended.

[8] See Von Kremer's *Culturgesch.*, ii, pp. 380, 381; Brockelmann's *Arab. Litt.*, pp. 86–89.

[9] See Brockelmann's *Arab. Litt.*, p. 253; and the *Yatíma*, vol. iv, pp. 25 and 62–64, where mention is made of two Abíwardís.

[10] Brockelmann, op. cit., p. 253. A., however, reads عزّى.

[11] See Ethé's monograph, and also his article on Rúdagí in the *Encyclopaedia Britannica*.

[12] See especially Noeldeke's *D. Iranische Nationalepos* in vol. ii (pp. 130–211) of Geiger and Kuhn's *Grundriss d. Iranischen Philologie*.

[13] See Ethé in the same *Grundriss*, pp. 224, 225.

[14] Abu'l-Qásim 'Alí b. Muḥammad al-Iskáfí. See *Yatíma*, vol. iv, pp. 29–33; iii, 4.

Anecdote ii.

Iskáfí was one of the secretaries of the House of Sámán, and knew his craft right well, so that he could cunningly traverse all obstacles, and emerge triumphant from the most difficult passes. He discharged the duties of secretary in the Chancellery of Núḥ b. Manṣúr,[1] but they did not properly recognize his worth, or bestow on him favours adequate to his pre-eminence. He therefore fled from Bukhárá to Alptagín at Herát. Alptagín, a Turk, wise and discerning, made much of him, and confided to him the Chancellery, so that at length he became one of his ministers. Now because there had sprung up at the court a new nobility who made light of the old nobles, while Alptagín patiently bore their presumption, matters at last culminated in rebellion, by reason of some slight put upon him. Then Amír Núḥ, incited by a party of the new nobles, wrote from Bukhárá to Zábulistán that Sabuktagín should come with that army, and the sons of Simjúr[2] with their army from Níshápúr, and should make war on Alptagín. And this war is very celebrated, and the event most notorious.

So when these armies reached Herát, the Amír 'Alí b. Muḥtáj[3] sent Kisá'í,[4] who was the Chief Chamberlain (*Ṣáḥibu'l-Báb*), to Alptagín, with a letter like fire and water blended together, containing threats and menaces which left no room for peace and no way for conciliation, such as an angry master might write in his absence to his disobedient

[1] This seems to be an error (though it stands thus in all three copies) for Manṣúr b. Núḥ (Manṣúr I), who reigned A.H. 350–366; for Núḥ b. Manṣúr (Núḥ II) reigned A.H. 366–387, and Alptagín died in A.H. 352 or 354. Concerning the *Díwánu'r-Rasá'il*, see Von Kremer's *Culturgeschicht. d. Arab.*, i. pp. 174, 200; and A. de B. Kazimirski's *Menoutchehri*, pp. 36 and 43. According to Ibnu'l-Athír (Búláq ed. of A.H. 1303, vol. viii, p. 179), Alptagín's revolt took place in A.H. 351.

[2] See Defrémery's *Hist. des Samanides*, pp. 260, 261.

[3] Concerning this general, see Defrémery's *Hist. des Samanides*, p. 243.

[4] A. has الكشای both here and in l. 4 of the next page, and in the second place adds *'Alí b. Muḥtáj* after *Abu'l-Ḥasan*.

servants, the whole letter filled with such expressions as "I will come," "I will take," "I will bind," "I will strike," "I will slay." When the Chamberlain Abu'l-Ḥasan Kisá'í submitted this letter and delivered the message, not withholding aught, Alptagín, who was already vexed, grew more vexed, and broke out in anger, saying: "I was his father's servant, but when my master passed from this transitory to that eternal abode, he entrusted him to me, not me to him. Although, to outward seeming, I should obey him, it is in fact quite otherwise, for when you examine this matter, a contrary conclusion results, seeing that I am in the last stages of old age, and he in the first stages of youth. Those who have impelled him to act thus are destroyers of this Dynasty, not counsellors, and are overthrowers of this house, not supporters."

Then he asked of Iskáfí, "How wilt thou answer this letter?" Iskáfí, on the spur of the moment, wrote the first draft of the answer as follows:—

"*In the Name of God, the Merciful, the Clement. O Núḥ, thou hast contended with us and made great the contention with us. Produce, then, that wherewith thou threatenest us, if thou art of those who speak truly.*"[1]

When this letter reached Núḥ b. Manṣúr, the Amír of Khurásán, he read it, and was astonished; and all the gentlemen of the court were filled with amaze, and the scribes bit their fingers in wonder. And when the affair of Alptagín was disposed of, Iskáfí fled away privily, for he was fearful and terrified; until suddenly Núḥ sent a messenger to him to summon him to his presence, and conferred on him the post of Secretary. So his affairs prospered, and he became conspicuous and famous amongst the votaries of the Pen. Had he not known the Qur'án, he would not thus have distinguished himself on this occasion, nor would his position have risen from the station he occupied to this high degree.

[1] Qur'án, xi, 34.

Anecdote iii.

When Iskáfí's affairs waxed thus prosperous, and he became established in the service of Núḥ b. Manṣúr, Mákán the son of Kákí[1] rebelled at Ray and in Kúhistán, withdrew his neck from the yoke of obedience, sent his agents to Khwár, Simnán and Simnák, captured several of the towns of Kúmish,[2] and paid no heed to the Sámánids. Núḥ b. Manṣúr was afraid, because this was a formidable and able man, and set himself to deal with this matter. He therefore ordered Tásh, the commander-in-chief, to march against him with seven thousand horsemen, suppress this sedition, and put an end to this grave incident in whatever way he deemed most expedient.

Now Tásh was very wise and clear in judgement, emerging swiftly and skilfully from the straitest passes; and he was also victorious in warfare, and had never turned back in defeat from any one of the countless battles he had waged, nor come forth worsted from any campaign. While he lived, the dominion and authority of the House of Sámán enjoyed the greatest brilliancy and prosperity.

On this occasion, then, the Amír, being much preoccupied and distressed, sent a messenger to summon Iskáfí, and held a private interview with him. "I am greatly troubled," said he, "by this occurrence; for Mákán is a brave man, and an able, and hath, in addition to his bravery and courage, administrative capacity and generosity, so that there have been few like him amongst the Daylamís. You must co-operate with Tásh, and whatever he lacks for the raising of an army at this juncture, you must supply.

[1] The chronological difficulties involved in these two stories are considerable, for the rebellion of Mákán b. Kákí occurred in A.H. 320, towards the end of the reign of Naṣr II b. Aḥmad, i.e. long before the rebellion of Alptagín (see n. 1 on p. 648, *supra*). See Defrémery's *Samanides*, pp. 248 and 263–4.

[2] Better known as *Qúmis*, the Arabicized form of the name. See B. de Meynard's *Dict. Géogr., Histor., et Litt. de la Perse*, pp. 464–5. For the three other towns mentioned, see the same work, pp. 213, 317, and 318.

And I will establish myself at Níshápúr, so that the army may be supported from the base, and the foeman discouraged. Every day a swift messenger must come from you to me with dispatches, wherein you must set forth the pith of what may have happened, so that my anxieties may be assuaged." Iskáfí bowed and said, "I will obey."

So next day Tásh unfurled his standard, sounded his drums, and set out for the front from Bukhárá, crossing the Oxus with seven thousand horsemen; while the Amír followed him with the remainder of the army to Níshápúr. There he invested Tásh and the army with robes of honour; and Tásh, raising his standard, marched into Bayhaq, whence he marched forwards into Kúmish to confront the enemy, with fixed purpose and in the best of spirits.

Meanwhile Mákán, with ten thousand mailed men, was encamped at the gates of Ray, where he had taken up his position. Tásh arrived, passed by the city, and encamped over against him. Then messengers passed to and fro between them, but no settlement was effected, for Mákán was puffed up with pride on account of that formidable army which he had gathered together from every quarter. It was therefore decided that they should join battle.

Now Tásh was an aged warrior, who for forty years had held the position of commander-in-chief, and had witnessed many such engagements; and he so manœuvred that when the two armies met, and the doughty warriors and champions of Transoxania and Khurásán moved forward from the centre, only half of Mákán's army was engaged, while the rest were not fighting. Mákán was slain, and Tásh, when he had ceased from taking and binding and slaying, turned to Iskáfí and said, "A carrier-pigeon must be sent in advance, to be followed later by a courier: but all the main features of the battle must be summed up in one sentence, which shall indicate all the circumstances, yet shall not exceed what a pigeon can carry, and shall adequately express our meaning."

Then Iskáfí took so much paper as two fingers would cover and wrote:—"*In the Name of God, the Merciful, the*

Clement. As for Mákán, he hath become as his name"[1] [*Má kán* = "He hath not been" in Arabic]. By this "*má*" he intended the negative, and by "*kán*," the verb substantive, so that the Persian of it would be, "Mákán hath become like his name," that is to say, hath become nothing.

When the carrier-pigeon reached the Amír Núḥ, he was not more delighted at the victory than at this dispatch, and he ordered Iskáfí's salary to be increased, saying: "Such a person must maintain a heart free from care in order to attain to such delicacies of expression."[2]

Anecdote iv.

One who pursues any craft which depends on reflection ought to be free from care and anxiety, for if it be otherwise, the arrows of his thought will fly wide and will not hit the target of achievement, since only by a tranquil mind can one arrive at such words.

It is related that a certain Secretary of the 'Abbásid Caliphs was writing a letter to the governor of Egypt; and, his mind being tranquil and himself submerged in the ocean of reflection, was forming sentences precious as pearls of great price and fluent as running water. Suddenly his maidservant entered, saying, "There is no flour left." The scribe was so put out and disturbed in mind that he lost the thread of his diction, and was so affected that he wrote in the letter "There is no flour left." When he had finished it, he sent it to the Caliph, having no knowledge of these words which he had written.

When the letter reached the Caliph, and he read it, and saw this sentence, he was greatly astonished, being unable to account for so strange an occurrence. So he sent a messenger to summon the scribe, and enquired of him

[1] ‹ امّا ماكان فصار كاسمه ›.

[2] The substance of this anecdote is given in the *Ta'ríkh-i-Guzída*, and is cited by Defrémery at pp. 247–8 of his *Histoire des Samanides* (Paris, 1845).

concerning this. The scribe was covered with shame, and gave the true explanation of the matter. The Caliph was mightily astonished and said: "The beginning of this letter excels the latter part by as much as the súra '*Say, He is God, the One*'[1] excels the súra '*The hands of Abú Lahab shall perish*,'[2] and it is a pity to surrender the minds of eloquent men like you into the hands of the struggle for the necessaries of life." Then he ordered him to be given means sufficiently ample to prevent such an announcement as this from ever entering his ears again. Naturally it then happened that he could compress into two sentences the ideas of two worlds.

Anecdote v.

The Ṣáḥib Isma'íl ibn 'Abbád,[3] entitled *al-Káfí* ("the Competent"), of Ray,[4] was minister to the Sháhansháh. He was most perfect in his accomplishments, of which fact his correspondence and his poetry are two sufficient witnesses and unimpeachable arbiters.

Now the Ṣáḥib was a man of just dealings, and such are wont to be extremely pious and scrupulous in their religious duties, not holding it right that a true believer should abide eternally in hell by reason of a grain of [righteous] enmity; and his servants and retainers and agents for the most part followed his example.

Now there was at Qum a judge appointed by the Ṣáḥib in whose godliness and piety he had the firmest belief, though there were some who asserted the contrary, and brought information against him, which, however, left the Ṣáḥib unconvinced, until certain trustworthy persons of Qum, whose statements commanded credence, declared that

[1] Qur'án, cxii.
[2] Qur'án, cxi.
[3] For an account of this great minister and generous patron of literature, see De Slane's translation of *Ibn Khallikán*, vol. i, pp. 212–217, and n. 4 on p. 030, *supra*.
[4] So B. Both A. and L. have الوادی.

in a certain suit between So-and-so and Such-an-one this judge had accepted a bribe of five hundred *túmáns*. This was mightily displeasing to the Ṣáḥib for two reasons, first on account of the greatness of the bribe, and secondly on account of the shameless unscrupulousness of the judge. He at once took up his pen and wrote:—

"*In the Name of God, the Merciful, the Clement. O Judge of Qum! We dismiss you, so Come!*"[1]

Scholars and rhetoricians will notice and appreciate the high merit of this sentence in respect of its brevity, concision, and clearness, and naturally from that time forth rhetoricians and stylists have inscribed this epigram on their hearts, and repeat it to the people of the world.

Anecdote vi.

Lamghán[2] is a city in the district of Sind, one of the dependencies of Ghazna; and at this present time naught but one range of mountains separates its inhabitants from the heathen, so that they live in constant dread of the attacks and raids of the unbelievers. Yet the men of Lamghán are of good courage, sharp and frugal, and combining with their sharpness no small rascality,[3] to such a degree that they think nothing of lodging a complaint against a tax-gatherer on account of a maund of chaff or a single egg; while for even less than this they were ready to come to Ghazna to complain of exactions, and would remain there one or two months, and then return without having accomplished their object. In short, they are wonderful hands at patience, and are most stiffnecked in importunity.

[1] ، بسم اللّه الرّحمن الرحيم ' ايها القاضى بقمّ ند عزلناك نقم '
I have endeavoured to preserve, feebly enough, the word-play in the original.

[2] Or Lámaghán. See B de Meynard's *Dict. Géogr. de la Perse*, p. 503; Pavet de Courteille's *Mém. de Baber*, ii, pp 120, 121.

[3] The texts differ considerably in this sentence. I follow A., which has:
امّا لمغانیان مردان بشکوه باشند و جلد و کسوب و با جلدی
زعری عظیم . . .

Now in the reign of Sulṭán Maḥmúd Yamínu'd-Dawla, the heathen one night attacked them, and damage of every sort befel them. But these were men who could raise a harvest without soil; and when this event happened several of their chiefs and men of note rose up and came to Ghazna, and, with their garments rent, their heads uncovered, and uttering loud lamentations, entered the bazaar of Ghazna, went to the King's Palace wailing and grieving, and so described their misfortune that even a stone would have been moved to tears. As their rascality, impudence, dissimulation, and cunning had not yet become apparent, that great minister, Aḥmad Ḥasan of Maymand,[1] took pity upon them, and forgave them that year's taxes, exempting them from all exactions, and bidding them return home, strive more strenuously, and spend less, so that by the beginning of the next year they might recover their former position.

So the deputation of Lamghánís returned with great contentment and huge satisfaction, and continued during that year in the easiest of circumstances, divulging their secret to no one.[2] When the year came to an end, the same deputation returned to present another petition to the minister, simply setting forth that in the past year their lord the great minister had brightened their country by his grace and clemency and had effectively extended to them his protection, so that they were now able to dwell in peace on that border; but that, since their prosperity was still somewhat shaken, they feared that, should he demand the contribution on their possessions that year, some of them would be utterly ruined, and that, as a consequence of this, loss might accrue to the royal coffers.

The minister, therefore, extending his favour, excused them the taxes of yet another year. During these two years the people of Lamghán grew rich, but this did not suffice them, for in the third year their greed reasserted

[1] See n. 4 on p. 25, *supra*.

[2] This I take to be the meaning of آب بکس ندادند.

itself, and, hoping again to be excused, the same deputation again appeared at Court and made a similar representation. Then it became apparent to all the world that the people of Lamghán were in the wrong. So the minister turned the petition over and wrote on the back of it: "*Al-kharáju khurájun, adá'uhu dawá'uhu,*" that is to say, "*The tax is a running sore: its cure is its discharge.*" And from the time of this great statesman this saying has become proverbial, and has proved useful in many cases. May the earth rest lightly on this great man!

Anecdote vii.

There were great statesmen under the 'Abbásid dynasty, and indeed the history of the Barmecides is well known and famous, and to what extent were their gifts and rewards. [Ibn] Sahl, called *Dhu'r-Riyásatayn*[1] ("the lord of two commands"), and his brother Faḍl were exalted above the very heavens, so much so that Ma'mún espoused Faḍl's daughter and asked her in marriage. Now she was a damsel peerless in beauty and unrivalled in attainments; and it was agreed that Ma'mún should go to the bride's house and remain there for a month, and after the lapse of this period return home with the bride. On the day fixed for their departure he desired, as is customary, to array himself in better clothes. Now Ma'mún always wore black; and people supposed that he wore it because black was the distinctive colour of the 'Abbásids: till one day Yaḥyá b. Aktham[2] inquired of him, "Why is it that the Prince of Believers prefers black garments?" Ma'mún replied to the Judge: "Black garments are for man and for the living; for no woman is married in black, nor is any dead

[1] There appears to be a confusion here between the two brothers. Ḥasan ibn Sahl was the father of Púrán, al-Ma'mún's bride, while Faḍl bore the title of *Dhu'r-Riyásatayn*. See De Slane's *Ibn Khallikán*, vol. i, pp. 268–272 and 408–409; vol. ii, pp. 472–475. Also the *Laṭá'ifu'l-Ma'árif* of ath-Tha'álibí (ed. De Jong), pp. 73, 74, where a full account is given of this marriage.

[2] See De Slane's *Ibn Khallikán*, iv, pp. 33–51.

man buried in black." Yaḥyá was greatly surprised by this answer. So on this day Ma'mún desired to inspect the wardrobe; but of a thousand coats of satin, of royal fabric, of fur, hand-woven, of various colours, hand-cut, of fine black silk,[1] he neither approved nor accepted one, but clad himself in his customary black, and mounted, and turned his face towards the bride's house. Now on that day Faḍl had decked out his palace in such wise that the nobles were filled with wonder thereat, for he had collected so many rare things that words would fail to describe or enumerate them. So when Ma'mún reached the gate of this palace, he saw a curtain suspended, fairer than a Chinese spring, and more delightful than the assurance of faith, whereof the design charmed the heart and the colour mingled with the soul; and he said to himself: "Whichever of those thousand coats I had chosen, I should have been shamed here. Praise be to God and thanks that I was content with this black raiment."

Now of all the elaborate preparations made by Faḍl on that day, one was this, that when Ma'mún reached the middle of the palace yard, he saw a tray filled with wax, round which was arranged a pattern of pearls.[2] And at the foot of each guest were cast several nuts, in each of which was a piece of paper whereon was inscribed the name of a village; and whoever drew one, to him were delivered the title-deeds of that village.

So when Ma'mún entered the bride's house, he saw a mansion faced with gypsum and adorned with paintings,[3]

[1] The exact nature of most of these fabrics I have been unable to ascertain. The list runs as follows: اطلس و ملکی و تُمَم [طمیم A., B.,] و نسیج و ممزّج و مقراضی و اکسون

[2] This sentence is not quite clear. It runs: طبقی [دید A., B. om.] پر کرده [بود L. om.] از موم بهیئت مروارید گرد کرده هریکی چند [چند A.] فندقی در پای او ریخت [ریختند L.].

[3] A., B have مجصّص و منقّش. L. reads: مخصّص.

strewn with perfumes of China, fairer than the East at the time of sunrise, and sweeter than a garden in the season of the rose. He saw, moreover, cast down and spread out at the entrance of the house, mats of cloth of gold,[1] embroidered with rubies, pearls, and turquoises; and in like manner six cushions placed thereon, on which was seated a bounteous damsel sweeter than existence and life, and pleasanter than health and youth; in stature such that the noble cypress would have subscribed itself her servant; with cheeks which the brightest sun would have acknowledged as suzerain; with hair which was the envy of musk and ambergris; and with eyes after the likeness of the onyx and the narcissus.[2] She, rising to her feet, advanced towards Ma'mún, with a profound obeisance and earnest apologies, brought him forward and seated him in the chief seat, and stood before him in service. Ma'mún bade her be seated, whereupon she seated herself on her knees,[3] hanging her head and looking down at the carpet. Thereupon Ma'mún was overcome with love: he had already lost his heart, and now he would have added thereunto his very soul. He stretched out his hand and drew forth from the pocket of his coat eighteen pearls, each one as large as a sparrow's egg, brighter than the stars of heaven, more lustrous than the teeth of the fair, rounder, nay, more luminous, than Jupiter or Saturn. These rolled on the surface of the carpet, and, by reason of its smoothness and their roundness, continued in motion, there being no cause for their quiescence. But the girl paid no heed to the pearls, nor so much as raised her head. Thereat was Ma'mún's passion further increased, and he extended

[1] This sentence, again, is not clear. It runs:

.. و خانه واری حصیر از شوشهٔ زر کشیده افگنده.

[2] A., B.: 'و چشم او از جسم جزع و عبهر بود.' L. has: 'و چشمی چون چشم حذع و عبهر'

[3] i.e., in the Persian fashion, on the heels, with the knees together in front.

his hand to caress her, and would have opened the door of amorous dalliance. But this caress aroused her modesty and covered her with confusion, and the delicate damsel was so affected that she was overtaken by that state peculiar to women, and the marks of shame and abashed modesty appeared in her cheeks and countenance, and she suddenly exclaimed: *"O Prince of Believers! The command of God cometh, seek not then to hasten it!"*[1]

Thereat Ma'mún withdrew his hand, and was near swooning on account of the extreme beauty of this citation, and her graceful application of it. Yet still he could not take his eyes off her, and for eighteen days he came not forth from this house and concerned himself with naught save two occupations. And the affairs of Faḍl prospered, and he attained to that high position to which he attained.

Anecdote viii.

Again in the time of the 'Abbásid Caliphs, in the reign of al-Mustarshid bi'lláh[2] (may God make his tomb fragrant and exalt his rank in Paradise!), the son of al-Mustaẓhir bi'lláh, the Prince of Believers came forth from the city of Baghdad with a well-equipped army in full panoply, and much treasure, and many muniments of war, marching against Khurásán, on account of a reparation which he would exact from the King of the World Sanjar.[3]

Now this quarrel had been contrived by interested persons, and was due to the machinations and representations of conspirators, who had brought matters to this pass. When the Caliph reached Kirmánsháh, he there delivered on a Friday a homily which in eloquence transcended the highest zenith of the sun, and reached the support and

[1] Qur'án, xvi, 1. Cf. De Slane's *Ibn Khallikán*, vol. i, p. 270.
[2] The twenty-ninth 'Abbásid Caliph, reigned A.H. 512–529.
[3] This happened in A.H. 529. See Houtsma's *Recueil de Textes relatifs à l'Histoire des Seldjoucides*, vol. ii (1889), pp. 171–178.

crown of the guard-stars.[1] In the course of this harangue, after expressing his distress and despair, he complained of the House of Seljúq, in such wise that the orators of Arabia and the rhetoricians of Persia have confessed that, after the companions of the Prophet (God's blessing and peace rest on him, and his family), who were the disciples of the Focus of the Prophetic Function and the expounders of his pithy aphorisms, no one had composed a discourse so weighty and eloquent. Said al-Mustarshid: "*We entrusted our affairs to the House of Seljúq, but they contended against us, and the time lengthened over them, and their hearts were hardened, and many of them sinned,*"[2] that is to say, withdrew their necks from our commands in the Religion of Islám.

Anecdote ix.

The Gúr Khán of Khitá fought a battle with the King of the World Sanjar, the son of Maliksháh, at the gates of Samarqand, and so fateful was the day to the army of Islám that Transoxania passed into his power.[3] After putting to death the Imám of the East Ḥusámu'd-Dín (may God make bright his example, and extend over him His Peace!), the Gúr Khán bestowed Bukhárá on Alptagín.[4] When the Gúr Khán turned back, he entrusted the son of the Amír Bayánání,[5] the nephew of Atsiz Khwárazmsháh,

[1] *Fargadayn*, two bright stars near the Pole-star, β and γ of Ursa Minor. See vol. ii of my *Traveller's Narrative*, p. 125, n. 2.

[2] فوّضنا أمورَنا الى آل سلجوق فبرزوا علينا فطال عليهم الامد فقست قلوبهم و كثيرٌ منهم فاسقون

[3] See Mírkhwánd's *History of the Seljúqs*, ed. Vullers, pp. 170–180. Professor Ross has pointed out to me that Gúr Khán is a generic title. See *History of the Moghuls of Central Asia*, by Elias and Ross, p. 287 et seqq. See also Schefer's *Chrestomathie Persane*, vol. i, p 34 et seqq.

[4] So L., agreeing with Schefer, op. cit., p. 29, where A.H. 536 is given as the date of this event. For *Alptagín* A. and B. read اتمتكين throughout.

[5] L. has ساماني, A. بياباني (uncertain), B. بياناني, but I cannot identify the name.

to the Imám Aḥmad b. 'Abdu'l-'Azíz, who was the Imám of Bukhárá, and the leading man of his time,[1] so that whatever he did he might do by his advice, and that he should not take any step without his instructions. Then the Gúr Khán turned back and retired to Bars-ján.[2]

Now his justice had no bounds, nor was there any limit to the effectiveness of his commands, and, indeed, in these two things lies the essence of kingship. But when Alptagín saw a clear field, he turned his hand to oppression, and began to levy contributions on Bukhárá. So several of the people of Bukhárá went as an embassy to the Gúr Khán[3] to seek redress. The Gúr Khán, after the way of good Muslims, wrote a letter in Persian to Alptagín as follows:—

"*In the Name of God, the Merciful, the Clement.* Let Alptagín know that, although wide distance separates us, our approval and displeasure are near at hand. Let Alptagín do that which Aḥmad commands, and Aḥmad that which Muḥammad commands. Farewell."

Again and again we have considered this and reflected on it. A thousand volumes or even more might be written to enlarge on this letter, yet its purport is extremely plain and clear, needing no explanation. Seldom have I seen anything like it.

Anecdote x.

The extreme eloquence of the Qur'án is in its concision of words and marvellous presentation of ideas; imitation thereof results but in citation, to such a degree that a sense

[1] For و پیشرو زمان, A. and B. have و پسر برهان, "and the son of Burhán."

[2] Name uncertain. L. has *Zanján*, which is quite unsuitable; A., به برسجان (not clearly legible); D., برسیکان.

[3] A. has, instead of نزد گورخان (L.'s reading), سوی برسجان; B., سوی برسیکان.

of awe is produced, and the wise and understanding man is converted from his state [of doubt]. And this is a clear proof and trenchant argument to establish the fact that this Word did not proceed from the mouth of any created being, nor issue from any human lips or tongue, but that the stamp of Eternity is the stigma of its prescriptions and sentences.

It is related that one day one of the Muslims was reciting before Walíd b. Mughíra this verse:—"*And it was said, 'O Earth, gulp down thy waters, and O Heaven, draw them up': and the water abated. Thus was the matter effected. And it [i.e. the Ark] rested upon Mount Júdí.*"[1] "By God," said Walíd b. Mughíra, "verily it hath beauty and sweetness, and verily at its highest it is terrible as a wild beast in fury, and at its lowest is as the deepest mine!"[2] When even enemies reached such a level of enthusiasm, by reason of the eloquence of the Qur'án and its incomparable height in the domain of religion and equity, to what degree must friends attain?

Anecdote xi.

In former times it was customary with the kings and tyrants of the world, such as the Píshdádí, Kayání, and Sásánian monarchs and the Caliphs, to vaunt themselves and compete with one another in justice and accomplishments, and with every ambassador whom they despatched they used to send wise sayings, riddles, and enigmatical questions. So the king, under these circumstances, stood in need of persons of intelligence and discrimination, and men of judgement and statesmanship; and several councils

[1] Qur'án, xi, 46.

[2] L. has ' انّ اعلاه منتثر و انّ اسفله لمعدن. In the margin لمغدق stands as a variant on لمعدن. A. and B. have لمعدق and مثمر for منتثر.

would be held and adjourned, until they were unanimous as to their answers, and when the inner meanings of these problems and enigmas were plain and apparent, then they would despatch the ambassador.

This practice was maintained until the time of Maḥmúd b. Sabuktagín Yamínu'd-Dawla (may God have mercy upon him!). One day he despatched an ambassador to Bughrá Khán in Transoxania, and in the letter which had been drafted occurred this passage:—"*God Almighty saith, 'Verily the most honourable of you in God's sight is he who is most pious of you.'*[1] The acute and critical are agreed that here he [i.e. the Prophet] guards himself from ignorance; for the souls of men are subject to no more grievous defect than this, nor is there aught lower than the fault of folly. To the truth of this proposition and the soundness of this assertion God's Word also bears witness: '*[God will raise up those of you who believe] and those to whom knowledge hath been given to [superior] degrees.*'[2] Therefore we desire that the Imáms of the land of Transoxania and the doctors of the East and scholars of the Kháqán's Court should give so much information touching essentials as to state what the Prophetic Office is, what Saintship, what Religion, what Islám, what Faith, what Well-doing, what Godliness, what the Approbation of Right, what the Prohibition of Wrong, what the Path, what the Balance, what Justice, and what Pity."

When this letter reached the Court of Bughrá Khán,[3] and he had acquainted himself with its purport and contents, he summoned the Imáms of Transoxania from the different towns and districts, informed them of the matter, and requested them to answer these words, bidding each one compose a treatise on this subject, and introduce in the course of their dissertation and argument a reply to these

[1] Qur'án, xlix, 13.
[2] Qur'án, lviii, 12.
[3] Here A. has غراخان and B قراخان, though they agree with L. above and below.

interrogations. They craved a delay of four months; which period dragged on with all sorts of detriments, the least of which was the disbursements from the treasury for the salaries of the ambassadors and the maintenance of the Imáms, until at length Muḥammad b. 'Abdu'lláh the scribe, who was Baghrá Khán's private secretary, and was deeply versed in learning and highly distinguished in scholarship, besides being one of the most eloquent stylists amongst the Muslims both in prose and verse, said: "I will answer these questions in two words, in such wise that when the greatest scholars and most conspicuous men of al-Islám shall see my answer, it shall command their approval and admiration." So he took up his pen and wrote under the questions, after the fashion of a legal decision (*fatwá*): "*Saith God's Apostle (upon whom be the Blessing of God, and also on his Family), 'Reverence for God's command and loving-kindness towards God's people.'*" All the Imáms of Transoxania bit their fingers in amazement and expressed their admiration, saying, "Here indeed is an answer which is perfect, and an utterance which is comprehensive!" And the Kháqán was mightily pleased because the difficulty had been overcome by a scribe and not left to the divines. And when the answer reached Ghazna, all applauded it.

It therefore results from these premises that an intelligent and accomplished Secretary is a great ornament to the brilliancy of a King's Court. And with this anecdote we conclude this chapter. And from God cometh assistance.

SECOND DISCOURSE.

On the Nature of Poetry, and the Utility of the Skilful Poet.

Poetry is that art whereby the poet arranges imaginary propositions, and adapts the deductions, with the result that he can make a little thing appear great and a great thing small, or cause good to appear in the garb of evil and evil in the garb of good. By acting on the imagination, he excites the faculties of anger and concupiscence in such a way that by his suggestion men's temperaments become affected with exultation or depression; whereby he conduces to the accomplishment of great things in the order of the world.

Anecdote xii.

Thus they relate that Aḥmad b. 'Abdu'lláh al-Khujistání[1] was asked, "How didst thou, who wert originally an ass-herd, become Amír of Khurásán?" He replied: "One day I was reading the Díván of Ḥandhala of Bádghís,[2] in Bádghís of Khujistán, when I chanced on these two couplets:—

'مهتری گر بکام شیر درست ' شو خطر کن ز کام شیر بجوی '
' یا بزرگی و ناز و نعمت و جاه ' یا چو مردانت مرگ رویاروی '

'If lordship lies within the lion's jaws,
Go, risk it, and from those dread portals seize
Such straight-confronting death as men desire,
Or riches, greatness, rank and lasting ease.'

An impulse stirred within me such that I could in no wise remain content with that condition wherein I was. I therefore sold my asses, bought a horse, and, quitting my country, entered the service of 'Amr b. Layth.[3] At that time the fortune of the Ṣaffárís still floated at the zenith of its prosperity. Of the three brothers, 'Alí was the youngest, and Ya'qúb and 'Amr had precedence over him.

[1] "Khujistan.—In the mountains near Herát. From this country issued Aḥmad b. 'Abdu'lláh al-Khujistání, who revolted at Níshápúr and died in A.H. 264." (Barbier de Meynard's *Dict. Géogr., Histor., et Litt. de la Perse*, p. 197.) The learned editor points out, however, that, according to Ibnu'l-Athír, Aḥmad was assassinated in the month of Shawwál, A.H. 268, after having reigned at Níshápúr for six years. See the *Journal Asiatique* for 1845, p. 345 et seqq. of the second half.

[2] See Ethé's *Rúdagí's Vorläufer und Zeitgenossen*, pp. 38–40, where these verses, and others by the same poet, are cited.

[3] Brother of Ya'qúb b. Layth, the founder of the short-lived Ṣaffárí dynasty. 'Amr reigned from A.H. 265 to A.H. 287.

When Ya'qúb came from Khurásán to Ghazna over the mountains, 'Alí b. Layth sent me back from *Ribáṭ-i-Sangín* ("the Stone Rest-house") to act as his agent to his feudal estates in Khurásán. I had collected an army of a hundred on the road, and had with me besides some twenty horsemen of my own. Now of the estates held in fief by 'Alí b. Layth one was Karúkh[1] of Herát, a second Khán-i-Níshápúr. When I reached Karúkh, I produced my warrant, and what was paid to me I divided amongst the army and gave to the soldiers. My horsemen now numbered three hundred. When I reached Khwáf,[2] and again produced my warrant, the burghers of Khwáf contested it, saying, 'Do we want a magistrate with [a bodyguard of only] ten men?'[3] I thereupon decided to renounce my allegiance to the Ṣaffárís, looted Khwáf, proceeded to the village of Yushh,[4] and came to Bayhaq, where two[5] thousand horsemen joined me. I advanced and took Níshápúr, and my affairs prospered and improved until all Khurásán lay open to me, and I took possession of it for myself. Of all this, these two verses of poetry were the cause."

Salámí[6] relates in his history that the affairs of Aḥmad b. 'Abdu'lláh prospered so greatly that in one night at Níshápúr he distributed in largesse 300,000 dínárs, 500 head of horses, and 1,000 suits of clothes, and to-day he

[1] See Barbier de Meynard's *Dict. Géogr., Hist., et Litt. de la Perse*, p. 467. B. and L. have "of Merv."

[2] Ibid., pp. 213, 214.

[3] The text and sense are both very doubtful. A. (f. 126) has گفتند مارا شحنهٔ باید با ده تن, while the lithograph has گفتند که مارا خواجه با دیه باید

[4] The MSS. have plainly بروستای یشب بیرون شدم, while the lithograph has و بشب بیرون شدم. I cannot, however, find mention of the village.

[5] The lithograph reads "a thousand."

[6] Concerning Ibn Salám, the author of a *Ṭabaqátu'sh-Shu'ará* (d. A.D. 845–6), who is probably intended, see J.R.A.S. for January, 1899, p. 48, footnote.

stands in history as one of the victorious monarchs, all of which was brought about by these two couplets of poetry. Many similar instances are to be found amongst both the Arabs and the Persians, but we have restricted ourselves to the mention of this one. So a king cannot dispense with a good poet, who shall conduce to the immortality of his name, and shall record his fame in *díwáns* and books. For when the king receives that command which none can escape,[1] no trace will remain of his army, his treasure, and his store; but his name will endure for ever by reason of the poet's verse, as Sharíf-i-Mujalladí of Gurgán says:—[2]

از آن چندان نعیم این جهانی ٭ که ماند از آل ساسان و آل سامان ٭
ثنای رودکی ماندست و مدحش ٭ نوای باربد ماندست و دستان ٭

"From all the treasures hoarded by the Houses
Of Sásán and of Sámán, in our days
Nothing survives except the song of Bárbad,
Nothing is left save Rúdagí's sweet lays."

The names of the monarchs of the age and the princes of the time are perpetuated by the admirable verse and widely-current poems of this guild; as, for instance, the names of the House of Sámán by Ustád Abú 'Abdi'lláh Ja'far b. Muḥammad *ar-Rúdakí*,[3] Abu'l-'Abbás b. 'Abbás[4] az-Zanjí, Abu'l-Mathal[5] al-Bukhárí, Abú Isḥaq Júybárí,[6] Abu'l-Ḥasan al-'Ají,[7] and Ṭabáwí, and Khabbází[8] of Níshápúr, and Abu'l-Ḥasan al-Kisá'í[9]; and the names of

[1] I.e., when he comes to die.
[2] B omits the poet's name altogether. L. has *Majdí*.
[3] al-'Awfí's *Lubáb*, part ii, No. 7.
[4] Ibid., No. 8, and Horn's ed. of the *Lughat-i-Asadí*, p. 24, first paragraph. L. has رازی and A. (f. 12*b*) زنجی.
[5] Ibid., No. 25, and Asadí, p. 28.
[6] Ibid., No. 10.
[7] The lithograph omits this name and the next; A. (f. 13*a*) has الاعجی, I suppose for العجی, "enfant nourri d'un lait étranger"; while B. has الاعجمی.
[8] 'Awfí, No. 29.
[9] See Ethé's monograph, *Die Lieder des Kisá'í*.

the kings of the House of Náṣiru'd-Dín [i.e. the Ghaznavids] by such men as 'Unṣurí, 'Asjudí, Farrukhí,[1] Bahrámí,[2] Zaynatí,[3] Buzurjmihr of Qá'in,[4] Mudhaffar,[5] Manshúrí,[6] Manúchihrí,[7] Mas'údí,[8] Qaṣárámí,[9] Abú Ḥanífa Iskáf ("the Cobbler"),[10] Ráshidí, Abu'l-Faraj of Rúna,[11] Mas'úd-i-Sa'd-i-Salmán,[12] Muḥammad Abú Naṣr,[13] Sháh Abú Rijá,[14] Aḥmad Khalaf, 'Uthmán Mukhtárí,[15] and Saná'í[16]; and the names of the House of Kháqán through Lúlú'í, Gulábí, Najíbí,[17] Farkhárí,[18] 'Am'aq of Bukhárá,[19] Rashídí of Samarqand,[20] Najjár ("the Carpenter")[21] -i-Ságharjí, 'Alí Pánídí,[22] the son of Darghúsh,[23] 'Alí

[1] Well-known contemporaries of Firdawsí. Mention is made of the first and last (of whose poems lithographed editions have been published at Ṭihrán) further on.

[2] Abu'l-Ḥasan 'Alí of Sarakhs. See *Majma'u'l-Fuṣaḥá*, vol. i, p. 173.

[3] Zaynatí-i-'Alawí-i-Maḥmúdí-i-Khurásání. See *M.F.*, vol. i, p. 241.

[4] Qásim b. Ibráhím b. Manṣúr. See *M.F.*, vol. i, p. 60.

[5] Or Mudhaffarí, of Panj-dih. See *M.F.*, vol. i, p. 505.

[6] Abú Sa'íd Aḥmad b. Muḥammad of Samarqand. See *M.F.*, vol. i, p. 600.

[7] See the edition of his *Díwán* by A. de Biberstein Kazimirski.

[8] Mas'údí of Ray (see *M.F.*, i, p. 503), another Ghaznavid poet, is apparently intended.

[9] L. substitutes *Ghaḍá'irí*. For Qaṣárámí see Horn's *Asadí*, p. 27.

[10] Of Merv or Ghazna. See 'Awfí's *Lubáb*, ch. x, No. 21, and *M.F.*, vol. i, pp. 83–85.

[11] See *M.F.*, i, pp. 70–78.

[12] Abu'l-Fakhr Mas'úd b. Sa'd b. Salmán of Ghazna (died A.H. 515 or 525). See Horn's *Lughat-i-Furs* of Asadí, p. 28, and *M.F.*, i, p. 514.

[13] L. has Majd-i-Náṣir. I can find no particulars concerning him.

[14] See *M.F.*, i, pp. 68–70. He was of Ghazna, and also bore the *laqab* of Shihábu'd-Dín.

[15] See Dawlatsháh's *Tadhkira* (pp. 93, 94 of my forthcoming edition), Ṭabaqa ii, No. 8.

[16] A. adds "Mawjúd," an error for "Majdúd." See Dawlatsháh (pp. 95–99), Ṭabaqa ii, No. 9; *M.F.*, i, pp. 254–274.

[17] L. omits this name and the next. Najíbu'd-Dín Jurbádhaqání (i.e. of Gulpáragán) is meant. See *M.F.*, i, pp. 634, 635.

[18] See Dawlatsháh (pp. 60, 70), Ṭabaqa i, No. 18.

[19] See Dawlatsháh (pp. 64–67), Ṭabaqa i, No. 15; *M.F.*, i, pp. 345–350.

[20] See Horn's *Asadí*, p. 18.

[21] See Anecdote xix, *infra*; and Horn's *Asadí*, p. 31.

[22] The second word is very uncertain. L. has تانبدی; A., تایندی, or تابیدی; B., ناپیدی; but lower (Anecdote xix), A. has بانیدی (i.e. پانیدی, or پانیذی), which I take to be the correct form.

[23] L. omits. B. has درغوشی. In both MSS. the first word is written بسر, which may stand for بشر, or possibly the correct reading is *Bashshár-i Marghazí*. See *M.F.*, i, p. 171.

Sipihrí,[1] Jawharí,[2] Sa'dí, the son of Tísha,[3] and 'Alí Shaṭranjí ("the Chess-player")[4]; and the names of the House of Seljúq by Farrukhí, Karkhání, Lámi'í of Dahistán,[5] Ja'far of Hamadán, Fírúzí-i-Fakhrí,[6] Burhání,[7] Amír Mu'izzí, Abu'l-Ma'álí of Ray,[8] 'Amíd Kamálí,[9] and Shiháb í[10]; and the names of the rulers of Ṭabaristán through Qamarí of Gurgán,[11] Ráfi'í of Níshápúr,[12] Kafáyatí[13] of Ganja, Kúsa Fálí, and Búrkala[14]; and the names of the kings of Ghúr, the House of Shansab (may God cause their rule to endure for ever!), through Abu'l-Qásim Rafí'í, Abú Bakr Jawharí, this least of mankind Niḏhámí-i-'Arúḍí, and 'Alí Ṣúfí. The *díwáns* of these poets are eloquent as to the excellence, comeliness, munitions and forces [of war], justice, bounty, worth, nobility, doughty deeds, judgement, statecraft, heaven-sent success and influence of these former kings, of whom to-day no trace remains, nor of their hosts and retinues any survivor. How many nobles there were under those dynasties who enjoyed the favours of kings, and dispensed untold largesses to these poets, and conferred on them sources of income, of whom to-day no trace remains; though many were the painted palaces and charming gardens which they created and embellished, but which to-day are

[1] See 'Awfí's *Lubáb*, ch. viii, No. 30; *M.F.*, i, pp. 244, 245; but the identity is uncertain.

[2] Called "the goldsmith" (*Zargar*). See Dawlatsháh (pp. 118–121). Ṭabaqa, ii, No. 18.

[3] Very doubtful. L. omits. A. has و بسر تبشه ; B., و برسید .

[4] Noticed in ch. x of 'Awfí's *Lubáb*; *M.F.*, i, pp. 314, 316.

[5] *M.F.*, i, pp. 491–501.

[6] Both MSS. have و در فیروز فخری .

[7] The father of Mu'izzí. Both are mentioned in Anecdote xvi, *infra*.

[8] *M.F.*, i, pp. 79, 80.

[9] Kamálu'd-Dín 'Amíd of Bukhárá. See *M.F.*, i, pp. 430, 437.

[10] Shihábu'd-Dín Aḥmad b. Mu'ayyad of Nasaf, near Samarqand. *M.F.*, i, pp. 310, 311.

[11] *M.F.*, i, pp. 477, 478.

[12] *M.F.*, i, pp. 220, 221.

[13] L. has كفائى .

[14] L. has Qá'iní for Fálí, and omits Búrkala.

levelled with the ground and uniform with the deserts and ravines! Says the author:—

بسا کاخا که محمودش بنا کرد ‘
که از رفعت همی با مه مرا کرد ‘

نه بینی زآن همه یک خشت بر پای ‘
مدیح عنصری ماندست بر جای ‘

"How many a palace did great Maḥmúd raise,
At whose tall towers the Moon did stand at gaze,
Whereof one brick remaineth not in place,
Though still re-echo 'Unṣurí's sweet lays."

When the Monarch of the World Sulṭán 'Alá'u'dunyá wa'd-Dín Abú 'Alí al-Ḥusayn b. al-Ḥusayn, the Choice of the Prince of Believers (may his life be long, and the umbrella of his dynasty victorious!) marched on Ghazna to avenge those two martyred kings and laudable monarchs,[1] whom Sulṭán Bahrámsháh had previously put to death after the fashion of common thieves, treating them with every indignity, and speaking lightly of them,[2] he sacked Ghazna, and destroyed the buildings raised by Maḥmúd, Mas'úd, and Ibráhím, but he bought with gold the poems written in their praise, and placed them in his library. In that army and in that city none dared call them king, yet he himself would read that *Sháhnáma* wherein Firdawsí says:—

[1] Quṭbu'd-Dín Muhammad and Sayfu'd-Dín Súri, both killed by Bahrámsháh the Ghaznavid, towards the middle of the sixth century of the Flight. From his devastation of Ghazna (A.H. 550, A.D. 1155–6) 'Alá'u'd-Dín Ḥusayn the Ghúrid received the title of *Jahán-súz* ("the World-consumer").

[2] This sentence is obscure in the first portion. It runs as follows in A.:—

خداوند عالم .... بکین خواستن آن دو ملک شهید و پادشاه حمید [که Lm] بغزنین رفت و سلطان بهرامشاه از پیش [او .A] برفت و در راه دزدان هر دورا شهید کردند و [که .A] استخفافها کرده بودند و گزافها گفته [و Im] غزنین را غارت کرد ....

چو کودک لب از شیر مادر بشست ، ز گهواره محمود گوید نخست ،

جهاندار محمود شاه بزرگ ، بآبشخور آرد همی میش و گرگ ،

> *"Of the child in its cot, ere its lips yet are dry*
> *From the milk of its mother, 'Maḥmúd!' is the cry!*
> *Maḥmúd, the Great King, who such order doth keep*
> *That in peace from one pool drink the wolf and the sheep!"*

All wise men know that herein was no reverence for Maḥmúd, but only admiration for Firdowsí and his verse. Had Maḥmúd understood this, he would probably not have left that noble man disappointed and despairing.

Excursus.

Now the poet must be of tender temperament, profound in thought, sound in genius, clear of vision, quick of insight. He must be well versed in many divers sciences, and quick to extract what is best from his environment; for as poetry is of advantage in every science, so is every science of advantage in poetry. And the poet must be of pleasing conversation in social gatherings, of cheerful countenance on festive occasions; and his verse must have attained to such a level that it is written on the page of Time and celebrated on the lips and tongues of the noble, and be such that they transcribe it in books and recite it in cities. For the richest portion and most excellent part of poetry is immortal fame, and until it be thus confirmed and published it is ineffectual to this end, and this result cannot accrue from it; it will not survive its author, and, being ineffectual for the immortalizing of his name, how can it confer immortality on another?

But to this rank a poet cannot attain unless in the prime of his life and the season of his youth he commits to memory

20,000 couplets of the poetry of the Ancients and 10,000 verses of the works of the Moderns, holds them constantly before his eyes, and continually reads and marks the *díwáns* of the masters of his art, observing how they have acquitted themselves in the strait passes and delicate places of song, in order that thus the fashion and varieties of verse may become ingrained in his nature, and the defects and beauties of poetry may be inscribed on the tablet of his understanding. In this way his style will improve and his genius will develop. Then, when his taste has been formed by wide reading of poetry, and his style of expression is thus strengthened, let him address himself seriously to the poetic art, study the science of Prosody, and peruse the works of Master Abu'l-Hasan Bahrámí of Sarakhs, such as the "Goal of Prosodists" (*Gháyatu'l-'Arúḍiyyín*), the "Thesaurus of Rhyme" (*Kanzu'l-Qáfiya*), and the works treating of poetic ideas and phraseology, plagiarisms, biographies, and all the sciences of this class, with such a master as he deemeth best, that thus he in turn may come to merit the title of Master, that his name may remain on the page of time like the names of those other Masters, which we have mentioned, and that he may be able to discharge his debt to his patron and lord for what he obtains from him, so that his name may endure for ever.

Now it behoves the King to patronize such a person, so that he may remain in his service and celebrate his praise. But if he fall below this level, he should waste no money on him and pay no heed to his poetry, especially if he be old; for I have investigated this matter, and in the whole world have found nothing worse than an old poet, nor any money more ill spent than what is given to such. For one so ignoble as not to have discovered in fifty years that what he writes is bad, when will he discover it? But if he be young and has the right talent, even though his verse be not good, there is some hope that it may improve, and according to the Law of Chivalry it is proper to patronize him, a duty to take care of him, and an obligation to maintain him.

Now in the service of kings naught is better than improvisation, for thereby the king's mood is cheered, his receptions are made brilliant, and the poet himself attains his object. Such favours as Rúdagí obtained from the House of Sámán by his improvisations and by virtue of his verse, none other hath experienced.

Anecdote xiii.

They relate thus, that Naṣr b. Aḥmad, who was the central point of the Sámánid group, whose fortunes reached their zenith during the days of his rule, was most plenteously equipped with every means of enjoyment and material of splendour—well-filled treasuries, an efficient army, and loyal servants. In winter he used to reside at Bukhárá, his capital, while in summer he used to go to Samarqand or some other of the cities of Khurásán. Now one year it was the turn of Herát. He spent the spring at Bádghís, where are the most charming pasture-grounds of Khurásán and 'Iráq, for there are nearly a thousand watercourses abounding in water and pasture, any one of which would suffice for an army.

When the beasts had well eaten, and had regained their strength and condition, and were fit for warfare or to take the field, Naṣr b. Aḥmad turned his face towards Herát, but halted outside the city of Marghazár-i-Sapíd and there pitched his camp. Cool breezes from the north were stirring, and the fruit was ripening in the districts of Málin and Karúkh[1]—fruit which can be obtained in but few places, and nowhere so cheaply. There the army rested. The climate was charming, the breeze cool, food plentiful, fruit abundant, and the air filled with fragrant scents, so that the soldiers enjoyed their life to the full during the spring and summer.

[1] See Barbier de Meynard's *Dict. de la Perse*, pp. 467, 511–512, according to which the former village is distant from Herát two parasangs, the latter ten.

When Mihrgán[1] arrived, and the juice of the grape came into season, and the eglantine, basil, and yellow rocket were in bloom, they did full justice to the charms of autumn, and took their fill of the pleasures of that season. Mihrgán was protracted, for the cold did not wax severe, and the grapes proved to be of exceptional sweetness. For in the district of Herát one hundred and twenty different varieties of the grape occur, each sweeter and more delicious than the other; and amongst them are in particular two kinds which are not to be found in any other region of the inhabited world, one called *Tarniyán*[2] and the other *Gulchidí*,[3] tight-skinned, slender-cored, and luscious, so that you would surely say they were [flavoured with] cinnamon.[4] A cluster of Gulchidí grapes sometimes attains a weight of five maunds; they are black as pitch and sweet as sugar, nor can one eat many for the sweetness that is in them. And besides these there were all sorts of other delicious fruits.

So the Amír Naṣr b. Aḥmad saw Mihrgán and its fruits, and was mightily pleased therewith. Then the narcissus began to bloom, and the raisins were plucked and stoned in Málin, and hung up on lines, and packed in chests; and the Amír with his army moved into the two groups of hamlets called Ghúra and Darwáz. There he saw mansions of which each one was like highest paradise, having before it a garden or pleasure-ground with a northern aspect. There they wintered, while the Mandarin oranges began

[1] The festival of the autumnal equinox, which fell in the old Persian month of Mihr.

[2] So L. B. has ترتیان , A. ﺑﺮﻧﻴﺎﻥ . The usual meaning of the word appears to be a sieve or basket made of osiers. See Horn's *Asadí*, p. 90, l. 1; Salemann's *Shams i Fachrii Lexicon*, p. 96, l. 13, and note *ad calc.*

[3] The reading is very uncertain. A. has کلجدی , L. کلاکجدی.

[4] Here also the reading is uncertain. I follow A., which seems to read: 'والبته گوئی که در [آن] دار صینی هستی . L. has: گوئی که درآن ارضی بسست'

to arrive from Sístán and the sweet oranges from Mázandarán; and so they passed the winter in the most agreeable manner.

When [the second] spring came, the Amír sent the horses to Bádghís and moved his camp to Málín [to a spot] between two streams. And when summer came, the fruits again ripened; and when Mihrgán came, he said, "Let us enjoy Mihrgán at Herát"; and so from season to season he continued to procrastinate, until four years had passed in this way. For it was then the heyday of the Sámánian prosperity, and the land was flourishing, the kingdom unmenaced by foes, the army loyal, fortune favourable, and heaven auspicious; yet withal the Amír's attendants grew weary, and desire for home arose within them, while they beheld the King quiescent, the air of Herát in his head and the love of Herát in his heart; and in the course of conversation he would declare that he preferred Herát to the Garden of Eden, and would set its charms above those of the springtide of Beauty.[1]

So they perceived that he intended to remain there for that summer also. Then the captains of the army and courtiers of the King went to Abú 'Abdu'lláh Rúdagí,[2] than whom there was none more honoured of the King's intimates, and none whose words found so ready an acceptance. And they said to him: "We will present thee with five thousand dínárs if thou wilt contrive some artifice whereby the King may be induced to depart hence, for our hearts are dying for desire of our wives and children, and our souls are like to leave us for longing after Bukhárá." Rúdagí agreed; and since he had felt the Amír's pulse and understood his temper, he perceived that prose would not affect him, and so had recourse to verse.

[1] So A., which reads بهار حسن; while L. has بهار چین, "a Chinese spring."

[2] See Ethé's excellent monograph, and his article in the *Encyclopaedia Britannica*, also p. 62 of the Journal for January, 1899.

He therefore composed a *qaṣída*; and, when the Amír had taken his morning cup, came in and did obeisance, and sat down in his place; and, when the musicians ceased, he took up the harp, and, playing the "Lover's air," began this elegy:—[1]

بوی جوی مولیان آید همی ، بوی یار مهربان آید همی ،

"The Jú-yi-Múliyán we call to mind,
We long for those dear friends long left behind."

Then he strikes a lower key, and sings:—

ریگ آمو و درشتی راه او ، زیر پایم پرنیان آید همی ،
آب جیحون از نشاط روی دوست ، خنگ ما را تا میان آید همی ،
ای بخارا شاد باش و دیر زی ، میر زی تو شادمان آید همی ،
میر ماهست و بخارا آسمان ، ماه سوی آسمان آید همی ،
میر سروست و بخارا بوستان ، سرو سوی بوستان آید همی ،

"The sands of Oxus, toilsome though they be,
Beneath my feet were soft as silk to me.
Glad at the friend's return, the Oxus deep
Up to our girths in laughing waves shall leap.
Long live Bukhárá! Be thou of good cheer!
Joyous towards thee hasteth our Amír!
The Moon's the Prince, Bukhárá is the sky;
O Sky, the Moon shall light thee by and bye!
Bukhárá is the mead, the Cypress he;
Receive at last, O Mead, thy Cypress-tree!"

[1] This poem is very well known, being cited in almost all notices of Rúdagí's life (e.g. by Dawlatsháh), in Forbes' *Persian Grammar*, pp. ۳۰, 2, 161–163, and in Blochmann's *Prosody of the Persians*, pp. 2–3.

When Rúdagí reached this verse, the Amír was so much affected that he descended from his throne, bestrode the horse which was on sentry-duty,[1] and set off for Bukhárá so precipitately that they carried his riding-boots after him for two parasangs, as far as Burúna,[2] and only then did he put them on; nor did he draw rein anywhere till he reached Bukhárá, and Rúdagí received from the army the double of that five thousand dínárs.

At Samarqand, in the year A.H. 504 (= A.D. 1110–1111), I heard from the Dihqán Abú Rijá Aḥmad b. 'Abdu'ṣ-Ṣamad al-'Ábidí as follows:—"My grandfather, the Dihqán Abú Rijá, related that [on this occasion] when Rúdagí reached Samarqand, he had four hundred camels laden with his wealth." And, indeed, that illustrious man was worthy of this splendid equipment, for no one has yet produced a successful imitation of that elegy, nor found means to surmount triumphantly the difficulties [which the subject presents]. Thus the Poet-laureate Mu'izzí was one of the sweetest singers and most graceful wits in Persia, and his poetry reaches the highest level in freshness and sweetness, and excels in fluency and charm. Zaynu'l-Mulk Abú Sa'd [b.] Hindú b. Muḥammad b. Hindú of Iṣfahán[3] requested him to compose an imitation of this *qaṣída*, and Mu'izzí, unable to plead his inability so to do, wrote:—

رستم از مازندران آید همی ' زین ملک از اصفهان آید همی '

"Now advanceth Rustam from Mázandarán,
Now advanceth Zayn-i-Mulk from Iṣfahán."

[1] *Khing-i-nawbatí.* To provide against any sudden emergency, a horse, ready saddled and bridled, was kept always at the gate of the King's palace, and it is this 'sentry-horse' to which reference is here made.

[2] L. has با برونه, and in a marginal note explains *burúna* as meaning turban or handkerchief; but A. has به برونه, and I suspect that it is really a place-name. Cf. Sachau's remarks on the derivation of al-Bírúní's name at p. 7 of his translation of the *Chronology of Ancient Nations*.

[3] See Houtsma's ed. of al-Bundárí's *History of the Seljúqs*, pp. 93, 101, 105.

All wise men will perceive how great is the difference between this poetry and that; for who can sing with such sweetness as does Rúdagí when he says:—

آفرین و مدح سود آید همی ' گر بگنج اندر زیان آید همی '

"Surely are renown and praise a lasting gain,
Even though the royal coffers loss sustain!"

For in this couplet are seven admirable touches of art: first, the verse is apposite; secondly, antithetical; thirdly, it has a refrain; fourthly, it embodies an enunciation of equivalence; fifthly, it has sweetness; sixthly, style; seventhly, energy. Every master of the craft, who has deeply considered the poetic art, will admit, after a little reflection, that I am right.

Anecdote xiv.

The love borne by Maḥmúd Yamínu'd-Dawla to Ayáz the Turk is well known and famous. It is related that Ayáz was not remarkably handsome, but had several good points. Of sweet expression and olive complexion, symmetrically formed, graceful in his movements, sensible and deliberate in action, he was mightily endowed with all the arts of courtiership, in which respect, indeed, he had few rivals in his time. Now these are all qualities which excite love and give permanence to friendship.

Now Maḥmúd was a pious and God-fearing man, and he wrestled with his love for Ayáz so that he did not diverge by so much as a single step from the Path of the Law and the Way of Chivalry. One night, however, at a carousal, when the wine had begun to affect him and love to stir within him, he looked at the curls of Ayáz, and saw, as it were, ambergris rolling over the face of the moon, hyacinths twisted about the visage of the sun, ringlet upon ringlet like a coat of mail; link upon link like a chain; in every ringlet a thousand hearts and under every look a hundred thousand souls. Thereupon love plucked the reins of self-restraint from the hands of his endurance, and lover-like he drew him to himself. But the watchman of "*Hath not God forbidden you to transgress against Him?*" thrust forth his head from the collar of the Law, stood before Maḥmúd, and said: "O Maḥmúd, mingle not sin with love, nor mix the false with the true, for such a slip will raise the Realm of Love in revolt against thee, and thou wilt fall like thy first father from Love's Paradise, and remain afflicted in the world of Sin." The ear of his fortunate nature being quick to hear, he hearkened to this announcement, and the tongue of his faith cried from his innermost soul, "*We believe and we affirm.*" Then, again, he feared lest the army of his self-control might be unable to withstand the evolutions of the locks of Ayáz, so, drawing a knife, he placed it in the hands of Ayáz, bidding him take it and cut off his curls. Ayáz took the knife from his hands with an obeisance, and, having enquired where he should cut them, was bidden to cut them in the middle. He therefore doubled back his locks to get the measurement, executed the King's command, and laid the two tresses before Maḥmúd. It is said that this ready obedience became a fresh cause of love; and Maḥmúd called for gold and jewels and gave to Ayáz beyond his usual custom and ordinary practice, after which he fell into a drunken sleep.

When the morning breeze blew upon him, and he arose from sleep to ascend the Royal Throne, he remembered what he had done. He summoned Ayáz and saw the clipped tresses. The army of remorse invaded his heart, and the peevish headache born of wine settled on his brain. He kept rising up and sitting down aimlessly, and none of the courtiers or men of rank dared to address to him any enquiry, until at length Ḥájib 'Alí Qaríb, who was the Chief Chamberlain, turned to 'Unṣurí and said, "Go, show thyself to him." So 'Unṣurí came in and did obeisance.

Maḥmúd raised his head and said: "I was just thinking of you. You see what has happened: say something on this subject." 'Unṣurí said:—

گر عیب سر زلف بت از کاستن است ٬
چه جای بغم نشستن و خاستن است ٬
جای طرب و نشاط و می خواستن است ٬
کآراستن سرو ز پیراستن است ٬

"Though shame it be a fair one's curls to shear,
Why rise in wrath or sit in sorrow here?
Rather rejoice, make merry, call for wine;
When clipped the cypress doth most trim appear."

Maḥmúd was highly pleased with this quatrain, and bade them bring gold and silver, which he mixed together, and therewith thrice filled the poet's lap. Then he summoned the minstrels before him, and drank wine to [the accompaniment of] those two verses whereby his melancholy had been dissipated, and recovered the equability of his temper.

Anecdote xv.

Now you must know that improvisation is the chief pillar of the Poetic Art; and it is incumbent on the poet to train his talents to such a point as to be able to improvise on any subject, for thus is money extracted from the treasury, and thus can the king be made acquainted with any matter which arises. All this is necessary to please the heart of one's patron and the humour of him who is the subject of one's eulogies; and whatever poets have earned in the way of great rewards has been earned by improvisations and poems inspired by the occasion.

Farrukhí was a native of Sístán, and was the son of Júlúgh,[1] the servant of Amír Khalaf.[2] He was possessed

[1] So A., but B. and L. read جولوغ, while *M.F.* has تلوغ.

[2] See Defrémery's *Histoire des Samanides*, p. 266.

of good talents, composed pleasing verses, and was a skilful performer on the harp; and he was retained in the service of one of the dihqáns of Sístán, who gave him a yearly allowance of two hundred measures of corn, each containing five maunds, and a hundred dirhams in silver coinage of Núḥ [which amply sufficed for his needs].[1] But he desired to marry a woman of Khalaf's clientage, whereby his expenses were increased, and the baskets and trays were multiplied,[2] so that Farrukhí remained without sufficient provision, nor was there in Sístán anyone else save[3] their amírs. He therefore appealed to the Dihqán, saying: "My expenses have been increased; how would it be if the Dihqán should make my allowance of corn three hundred maunds, and raise my salary by five hundred dirhams, so that my means may perhaps become equal to my expenditure?" The Dihqán wrote on the back of the appeal: "So much shall not be refused you, but there is no possibility of any further increase."

So Farrukhí was in despair, and made enquiries of such as arrived and passed by to hear of some patron in some region or part of the world who might look upon him with favour, so that he might chance on a success; until at length they informed him that the Amír Abu'l-Mudhaffar Chighání in Chigháníyán[4] was a munificent patron of this class, conferring on them splendid presents and rewards, and was at that period conspicuous in this respect amongst the kings of the age and nobles of the time. On the subject of this choice Farrukhí says:—

با کاروان حلّه برفتم زسیستان ٬ با حُلّهٔ تنیده زدل بافته زجان ٬

[1] The words و اورا تمام بودی are omitted by L.

[2] A. ٬ وکبه و زنبیل افزود.

[3] L. has از for مگر, so that the sense would then be "anyone of their amírs."

[4] Or, in its Arabicized form, *Ṣighániyán*, a place in Transoxania, near Tirmidh and Qubádhiyán. See De Goeje's *Bibl. Geogr. Arab.*, where it is mentioned repeatedly.

"*In a caravan of merchandise from Sístán did I start,*
With fabrics spun within my brain and woven by my heart."

In truth it is a fine elegy that he composed on the Poetic Art, incomparable in the beauty of its eulogies.

So Farrukhí, having furnished himself with what was necessary for the journey, set out for Chigháaniyán. Now Abu'l-Mudhaffar had 18,000 mares, roadsters,[1] each one of which was followed by its colt. And every year the Amír used to go out to brand the mares, and at this moment he happened to be at the place where the branding was done; while 'Amíd As'ad, who was his steward, was at the capital preparing provisions to be conveyed to the Amír. To him Farrukhí went, and recited a *qaṣída*, and submitted to him the poetry he had composed for the Amír.

Now 'Amíd As'ad was a man of parts and a poet, and in Farrukhí's verse he recognized poetry at once fresh, sweet, pleasing, and masterly, while seeing the man himself to be ill-proportioned, clothed in a torn jubba worn anyhow,[2] with a huge turban on his head after the manner of the Sagzís, of the most unprepossessing appearance from head to foot; and this poetry, withal, in the seventh heaven. He could not believe that it had been composed by this Sagzí, and, to prove him, said: "The Amír is at the branding-ground, whither I go to wait upon him; and thither I will take thee also, for it is a mighty pleasant spot—

جهانی در جهانی سبزه بینی '

'*World within world of verdure wilt thou see*'—

full of tents and lamps like stars, and from each tent come the songs of Rúdagí, and friends sit together, drinking wine and making merry, while before the Amír's pavilion a great fire is kindled, in size like unto several mountains,

[1] The word is راهی, explained in the margin of L as meaning گردنده و دونده '

[2] *Pish u pas.*

whereat they brand the colts. And the King, with the goblet in one hand and the lassoo in the other, drinks wine and gives away horses. Compose, now, a *qaṣída*, describing the branding-ground, so that I may take thee before the Amír."

That night Farrukhí went and composed the following *qaṣída*, which he brought before 'Amíd:—[1]

چون پرند نیلگون بر روی پوشد مرغزار ،
پرنیان هفت رنگ اندر سر آرد کوهسار ،
خاک را چون ناف آهو مشک زاید بیقیاس ،
بید را چون پر طوطی برگ روید بیشمار ،
دوش وقت نیم شب بوی بهار آورد باد ،
حبّذا باد شمال و خرّما بوی بهار ،
باد گوئی مشک سوده دارد اندر آستین ،
باغ گوئی لعبتان جلوه دارد در کنار ،
نسترن لولوی بیضا دارد اندر مرسله[2] ،
ارغوان لعل بدخشی دارد اندر گوشوار ،
تا بر آمد جامهای سرخ مل بر شاخ گل ،
پنجه‌ها چون دست مردم سر فرو کرد از چنار ،
باغ بو قلمون لباس و شاخ بو قلمون نمای ،
آب مروارید گون و ابر مروارید بار ،

[1] See pp. 114–117 of the lithographed edition of Farrukhí's works published at Ṭihrán for Mírzá Mahdí Khán *Badáyi'-nigár*, poetically surnamed Mukhliṣ, in A.H. 1301. Of the 52 bayts there given, only 22 are cited in the *Chahár Maqála*. The poem is also given by Dawlatsháh (pp. 55–57 of my forthcoming edition). Only a few of the more important variants are noticed here.

[2] A gloss in the lithographed Ṭihrán edition explains this word as meaning 'necklace' (گردن بند).

راست پنداری که خلعتهای رنگین یافتند
باغهای پر نگار از داغگاه شهریار
داغگاه شهریار اکنون چنان خرم شود
کاندرو از خرمی خیره بماند روزگار
سبزه اندر سبزه بینی چون سپهر اندر سپهر
خیمه اندر خیمه بینی چون حصار اندر حصار
سبزه ها پر بانگ چنگ و مطربان چرب دست
خیمه‌ها با بانگ نوش و ساقیان میگسار
هر کجا خیمه است خفته عاشقی با دوست مست
هر کجا سبزه است شادان یاری از دیدار یار
عاشقان بوس و کنار و نیکوان ناز و عتاب
مطربان رود و سرود و خفتگان خواب و خمار
بر در پرده سرای خسرو پیروز بخت
از پی داغ آتشی افروخته خورشید وار
بر کشیده آتشی چون مطرد دیبای زرد
گرم چون طبع جوان و زرد چون زر عیار
داغها چون شاخهای بسد یاقوت رنگ
هر یکی چون ناردانه گشته اندر زیر نار
بردگان[1] خواب نا دیده مصاف اندر مصاف
مرکبان داغ نا کرده قطار اندر قطار
خسرو فرخ سیر بر بارهٔ دریا گذر
با کمند اندر میان دشت چون اسفندیار

[1] L. has ریدگان glossed in the margin as 'slave-boys' (غلام بچگان). The Tihrán ed. has دیدگان, 'eyes.'

همچو زلف دلبران خورد ساله تاب خورد ،
همچو شهد دوستان سالخورده استوار ،
میر عادل[1] بو المظفّر شاد با پیوستگان ،
شهریار شیرگیر و پادشاه شهردار[2] ،
اژدها کردار پیچان در کف رادش کمند ،
چون عصای موسوی در دست موسی گشته مار ،
هر کرا اندر کمند شصت یازی در فگند ،
گشت نامش[3] بر سرین و شانه و رویش نگار ،
هرچه زین سو داغ کرد از سوی دیگر میدهد[4] ،
شاعران را با لگام و زایران را با فسار ،

"Since the meadow hides its face in satin shot with greens and blues,
And the mountains wrap their brows in silken veils of seven hues,
Earth is teeming like the musk-pod with aromas rich and rare,
Foliage bright as parrot's plumage doth the graceful willow wear.
Yestere'en the midnight breezes brought the tidings of the spring:
Welcome, O ye northern gales, for this glad promise which ye bring!
Up its sleeve the wind, meseemeth, pounded musk hath stored away,
While the garden fills its lap with shining dolls, as though for play.

[1] L. substitutes '*Fakhr-i-Dawlat.*'

[2] The Tihrán ed. has: 'شادمان و شادخوار و کامران و کامکار.

[3] So A. L. has داغش.

[4] So A. and L. The ed. has 'هدیه داد.

On the branches of syringa necklaces of pearls we see,
Ruby earrings of Badakhshán sparkle on the Judas-tree.
Since the branches of the rose-bush carmine cups and beakers bore
Human-like five-fingered hands reach downwards from the sycamore.
Gardens all chameleon-coated, branches with chameleon whorls,
Pearly-lustrous pools around us, clouds above us raining pearls!
On the gleaming plain this coat of many colours doth appear
Like a robe of honour granted in the court of our Amír.
For our Prince's Camp of Branding stirreth in these joyful days,
So that all this age of ours in joyful wonder stands agaze.
Green within the green you see, like skies within the firmament;
Like a fort within a fortress spreads the army, tent on tent.
Every tent contains a lover resting in his sweetheart's arms,
Every patch of grass revealeth to a friend a favourite's charms.
Harps are sounding 'midst the verdure, minstrels sing their lays divine,
Tents resound with clink of glasses as the pages pour the wine.
Kisses, claspings from the lovers; coy reproaches from the fair;
Wine-born slumbers for the sleepers, while the minstrels wake the air.
Branding fires, like suns ablaze, are kindled at the spacious gate
Leading to the State-pavilion of our Prince so fortunate.
Leap the flames like gleaming lances draped with yellow-lined brocade,
Hotter than a young man's temper, yellower than gold assayed.
Branding tools like coral branches ruby-tinted glow amain
In the fire, as in the ripe pomegranate glows the crimson grain.
Rank on rank of active boys, whose watchful eyes no slumber know;
Steeds which still await the branding, rank on rank and row on row.
On his horse, the river-forder, roams our genial Prince afar,
Ready to his hand the lassoo, like a young Isfandiyár.
Like the locks of pretty children see it how it curls and bends,
Yet be sure its hold is stronger than the covenant of friends.

Bu'l-Mudhaffar Sháh the Just, surrounded by a noble band,
King and conqueror of cities, brave defender of the land.
Serpent-coiled in skilful hands fresh forms his whirling noose doth take,
Like unto the rod of Moses metamorphosed to a snake.
Whosoever hath been captured by that noose and circling line,
On the face and flank and shoulder ever bears the Royal sign.
But, though on one side he brands, he giveth also rich rewards,
Leads his poets with a bridle, binds his guests as though with cords."

When 'Amíd As'ad heard this elegy, he was overwhelmed with amazement, for never had the like of it reached his ears. He put aside all his business, mounted Farrukhí on a horse, and set out for the Amír, whose presence he entered about sundown, saying: "O Sire, I bring thee a poet the like of whom the eye of Time hath not seen since Daqíqí's face was veiled in death." Then he related what had passed.

So the Amír accorded Farrukhí an audience, and when he came in he did reverence, and the Amír gave him his hand, and assigned him an honourable place, enquiring after his health, treating him with kindness, and inspiring him with hopes of favours to come. When the wine had gone round several times, Farrukhí arose, and, in a sweet and plaintive voice, recited his elegy, beginning:—

با کاروان حلّه برفتم ز سیستان ' با حلّهٔ تنیده ز دل بافته ز جان '

"In a caravan of merchandise from Sístán did I start,
With fabrics spun within my brain and woven in my heart."

When he had finished, the Amír, himself something of a poet, expressed his astonishment at this *qaṣída*. 'Amíd As'ad said, "Wait till you see!" Farrukhí was silent until the wine had produced its full effect on the Amír, then he arose and recited this elegy on the branding-ground. The Amír was amazed, and in his admiration turned to Farrukhí, saying: "They have brought in a thousand colts, all with white foreheads, fetlocks, and feet. Thou art a cunning rascal, a Sagzí; catch as many as thou art able, that they may be thine." Farrukhí, on whom the wine had produced its full effect, came out, took his turban from his head, hurled himself into the midst of the herd, and chased a drove of them before him across the plain; but, though he caused them to gallop hither and thither, he could not catch a single one. At length a ruined rest-house situated on the edge of the camping-ground came into view, and thither the colts fled. Farrukhí, being tired out, placed his turban under his head in the porch of the rest-house, and at once went to sleep, by reason of his extreme weariness and the effects of the wine. When they counted the colts, they were forty-two in number. The Amír, on being told of this, laughed and said: "He is a lucky fellow, and will come to great things. Look after him, and look after the colts as well. When he awakes, waken me too." So they obeyed the King's orders.

Next day, after sunrise, Farrukhí arose. The Amír had already risen, and, when he had performed his prayers, he gave Farrukhí an audience, treated him with great consideration, and handed over the colts to his attendants. He also ordered Farrukhí to be given a horse and equipments suitable to a man of rank, as well as a tent, three camels, five slaves, wearing apparel, and carpets. So Farrukhí prospered in his service, and enjoyed the greatest circumstance, and waited upon Sulṭán Maḥmúd, who, seeing him thus magnificently equipped, regarded him with the same regard, and his affairs reached that pitch of prosperity which they reached, so that twenty servants, girt with silver girdles rode behind him.

Anecdote xvi.

In the year A.H. 510 (A.D. 1116–1117) the King of Islám Sanjar, the son of Malikshāh the Seljúq (may God be merciful to him!), chanced to be encamped at the spring season within the marches of Ṭús, in the plain of Tarúq, when I, in hopes of obtaining some favour, joined his Court from Herát, having then nothing in the way of equipment or provision. I composed a *qaṣída* and went to Mu'izzí, the Poet-laureate, to seek for his counsel and support. He looked at my poem, and, having tested my talents in several ways, behaved in the most noble manner, and deemed it his duty to act in the way befitting so great a man.

One day I expressed in his presence a hope that Fortune would be more favourable to me, and complained of my luck. He answered genially: "Thou hast laboured hard to acquire this science, and hast fully mastered it: surely this will have its effect. My own case was precisely similar; and good poetry has never yet been wasted. Thou hast a goodly share in this art: thy verse is even and melodious, and is still improving. Wait and see the advantages which thou wilt reap from this science. For though Fortune should at first be grudging, matters will eventually turn out as thou wishest.

"My father Burhání, the Poet-laureate (may God be merciful to him!), passed away from this transitory to that eternal world in the town of Qazwín in the early part of the reign of Malikshāh, entrusting me to the King in this verse, since then become famous:—[1]

'من رفتم و فرزند من آمد خلف صدق ' اورا بخدا و بخداوند سپردم '

'I am flitting, but I leave a son behind me,
And commend him to my God and to my King.'

"So my father's salary and allowances were transferred to me, and I became Malikshāh's court-poet, and spent a year in the King's service; yet was I unable to see him save from a distance, nor did I get one dínár of my salary

[1] This verse, to which are added several others, is commonly ascribed to the Niḍhámu'l-Mulk, e.g. by Dawlatsháh (p. 59 of my forthcoming edition). Apart from the improbability that one who lay dying of a mortal wound would be in the mood to compose verses, we learn from this anecdote that the Niḍhámu'l-Mulk "had no opinion of poets because he had no skill in their art." The verse which gives his age as 84 at the time of his death (he was actually 80 at most) is alone enough to discredit the story.

or one maund of my allowances, while my expenditure was increased, I became involved in debt, and my brain was perplexed by my affairs. For that great Minister the Nidhámu'l-Mulk (may God be merciful to him!) had no opinion of poets, because he had no skill in their art; nor did he pay any attention to any one of the religious leaders or mystics.

"One day—it was the eve of the day on which the new moon of Ramadán was due to appear, and I had not a farthing for all the expenses incidental to that month and the feast which follows it—I went thus sad at heart to the Amír 'Alí Farámarz[1] 'Alá'u'd-Dawla, a man of royal parentage, a lover of poetry, and the intimate companion and son-in-law of the King, with whom he enjoyed the highest honour and before whom he could speak boldly, for he held high rank under that administration. And he had already been my patron. I said: 'May my lord's life be long! Not all that the father could do can the son do, nor does that which accrued to the father accrue to the son. My father was a bold and energetic man, and was sustained by his art, and the martyred King Alp Arslán, the lord of the world, entertained the highest opinion of him. But what he could do that can I not, for modesty forbids me. I have served this prince for a year, and have contracted debts to the extent of a thousand dinárs, and have not received a farthing. Crave permission, then, for thy servant to go to Níshápúr, and discharge his debts, and live on that which is left over, and express his gratitude to this victorious Dynasty.'

"'Thou speakest truly,' replied Amír 'Alí: 'we have all been at fault, but this shall be so no longer. The King, at the time of Evening Prayer, will go up to look for the moon. Thou must be present there, and we will see what Fortune will do.' Thereupon he at once ordered me to receive a hundred dínárs to defray my Ramadán expenses,

[1] Probably 'Alí b. Farámarz the Kákwayhid is intended. See Lane's *Muhammadan Dynasties*, p. 145.

and a purse containing this sum in Níshápúr coinage was forthwith brought and placed before me. So I returned mightily well pleased, and made my preparations for Ramaḍán, and at the time of the second prayer went to the King's pavilion. It chanced that 'Alá'u'd-Dawla arrived at the very same moment, and I paid my respects to him. 'Thou hast done excellently well,' said he, 'and hast come punctually.' Then he dismounted and went in before the King.

"At sundown the King came forth from his pavilion, with a cross-bow in his hand and 'Alá'u'd-Dawla on his right hand. I ran forward to do obeisance. Amír 'Alí continued the kindnesses he had already shown me, and then busied himself in looking for the moon. The King, however, was the first to see it, whereat he was mightily pleased. Then 'Alá'u'd-Dawla said to me, 'O son of Burhání, say something appropriate,' and I at once recited these two couplets:—

ای ماه چو ابروان یاری گوئی ، یا نی چو کمان شهریاری گوئی ،
نعلی زده از زر عیاری گوئی ، بر گوش سپهر گوشواری گوئی ،

'Methinks, O Moon, thou art our Prince's bow,
Or his curved eyebrow, which doth charm us so,
Or else a horse-shoe wrought of gold refined,
Or ring from Heaven's ear depending low.'

"When I had submitted these verses, Amír 'Alí applauded, and the King said: 'Go, loose from the stable whichever horse thou pleasest.' When I was close to the stable, Amír 'Alí designated a horse which was brought out and given to my attendants, and which proved to be worth 300 dínárs of Níshápúr. The King then went to his oratory, and I performed the evening prayer, after which we sat down to meat. At the table Amír 'Alí said: 'O son of Burhání! Thou has not yet said anything about this favour conferred on thee by the lord of the world. Compose a quatrain at once!' I thereupon sprang to my feet and recited these two verses:—

'چون آتش خاطر مرا شاه بدید
'از خاک مرا بر زبر ماه کشید
'چون آب یکی ترانه از من شنید
'چون باد یکی مرکب خاصم بخشید

'The King beheld the fire *which in me blazed:*
Me from low earth *above the moon he raised:*
From me a verse, like water *fluent heard,*
And swift as wind *a noble steed conferred.'*

"When I recited these verses 'Alá'u'd-Dawla warmly applauded me, and by reason of his applause the King gave me a thousand dinárs. Then 'Alá'u'd-Dawla said: 'He hath not yet received his salary and allowances. To-morrow I will sit by the Minister until he writes a draft for his salary on Isfahán, and orders his allowances to be paid out of the treasury.' Said the King: 'Thou must do it, then, for no one else has sufficient boldness. And call this poet after my title.' Now the King's title was *Mu'izzu'd-Dunyá wa'd-Dín*, so Amír 'Ali called me *Mu'izzí*. '*Amír* Mu'izzí,' said the King, [correcting him]. And this noble lord was so zealous for me that next day, by the time of the first prayer, I had received a thousand dínárs as a gift, twelve hundred more as allowances, and an order for a thousand maunds of corn. And when the month of Ramaḍán was past, he summoned me to a private audience, and caused me to become the King's boon-companion. So my fortune began to improve, and thenceforth he made enduring provision for me, and to-day whatever I have I possess by the favour of that Prince. May God, blessed and exalted is He, rejoice his dust with the lights of His Mercy, by His Favour and His Grace!"

Anecdote xvii.

The House of Saljúq were all fond of poetry, but none more so than Ṭughán Sháh b. Alp Arslán,[1] whose conversation and intercourse was entirely with poets, and whose favourite companions were almost all of this class—men such as Amír Abú 'Abdu'lláh Qurashí, Abú Bakr Azraqí,[2] Abú Manṣúr, Abú Yúsuf, Shujá'í of Fasá, Aḥmad Badíhí,[3] Ḥaqíqí and Nasímí, all of whom enjoyed a definite status, while many others kept coming and going, all departing with gifts and joyful countenances.

One day the King was playing backgammon with Aḥmad Badíhí. They were finishing a game for [a stake of] ten thousand [dínárs], and the Amír had two pieces in the sixth house and Aḥmad Badíhí two pieces in the first house[4]; and it was the Amír's throw. He threw with the most deliberate care, in order to cast two sixes, instead of which he threw two ones, whereat he was mightily vexed and left the board, while his anger rose so high and reached such a pitch that each moment he was like to put his hand to his sword, and his courtiers trembled like the leaves of a tree, seeing that he was a king, and withal a boy angered at such spite of Fortune.

Then Abú Bakr Azraqí arose, and, approaching the minstrels, recited this quatrain:—

گر شاه دو شش خواست دو یک زخم افتاد '

تا ظن نبری که کعبتین داد نداد '

[1] Called by Riḍá-qulí Khán (*M.F.*, i, 139) Ṭughánsháh b. Malik-i-Mu'ayyad. See Houtsma's *Hist. des Seljoucides de Kermán*, pp. 111, 119, 142.

[2] 'Awfí's *Lubáb*, ch. x, No. 3; Dawlatsháh (pp. 72-73 of my ed.), Ṭabaqa ii, No. 1; and *M.F.*, vol. i, pp. 139-152.

[3] *M.F.*, i, p. 169. His *laqab* was Majdu'd-Dín and his *nisba* Sajáwandí.

[4] For the explanation of this passage I am indebted to my friend Mírzá 'Abdu'l-Ghaffár of the Persian Legation. The six 'houses' on each side of the backgammon board are named (proceeding from left to right) as follows: (1) *khál-khána* or *yak-gáh*, (2) *dú-khán*, (3) *sí-khána*, (4) *chahár-khána*, (5) *panj-dar*, (6) *shash-khána* or *shash-dar-gáh*. The numbers contained in these names allude to the numbers which must be thrown with the dice to get the pieces which occupy them off the board.

آن زخم که کرد رای شاهنشه یاد ‘
در خدمت شاه روی بر خاک نهاد ‘

"Reproach not Fortune with discourteous tricks
If by the King, desiring double six,
Two ones were thrown; for whomsoe'er he calls
Face to the earth before him prostrate falls."

When I was at Herát in the year A.H. 509 (A.D. 1115–1116), Abú Manṣúr and Abú Yúsuf related to me that the Amír Tughánsháh was so charmed and delighted with these two verses that he kissed Azraqí on the eyes, called for gold, and successively placed five hundred dínárs in his mouth, continuing thus to reward him so long as one gold piece was left. Thus did he recover his good humour and such largesse did he bestow, and the cause of all this was one quatrain. May God Almighty have mercy on both of them, by His Favour and Grace!

Anecdote xviii.

In the year A.H. 472 (A.D. 1079–1080)[1] a certain spiteful person laid a statement before Sulṭán Ibráhím to the effect that his son, Maḥmúd Sayfu'd-Dawla, intended to go to 'Iráq to Maliksháh. The King's jealousy was aroused, and it so worked on him that suddenly he had his son seized, bound, and interned in the fortress of Náy. His son's intimates also he arrested and interned, amongst them Mas'úd-i-Sa'd-i-Salmán, whom he sent to Vajíristán,[2] to

[1] The two MSS. and L. all have "572," an evident error, for (1) Sulṭán Ibráhím the Ghaznavid reigned A.H. 451–492 (A.D. 1059–1099); (2) Maliksháh reigned A.H. 465–485 (A.D. 1072–1092), (3) the poet in question died in A.H. 515 or 525 (A.D. 1121 or 1130); (4) the *Chahár Maqála*, as we have already seen, was written during the lifetime of Sulṭán 'Alá'u'd-Dín Ḥusayn *Jahánsúz*, i.e. before A.H. 556 (A.D. 1161).

[2] So A., L.: B. has اورا ابو جبرستان. I cannot identify the word, and suspect that the reading is wrong.

the Castle of Náy; whence he sent to the King the following quatrain which he had composed:—

در بند تو ای شاه ملکشه باید ' تا بند تو پای تاجداری ساید '
آن کس که ز پشت سعد سلمان آید ' گر زهر شود ملک ترا بگزاید '

" O King, 't is Malikshúh should wear thy chain,
That royal limbs might fret with captive's pain,
But Sa'd-i-Salmán's offspring could not hurt,
Though venomous as poison, thy domain!"

'Alí Kháṣṣ brought this quatrain to the King, but it produced no effect on him, though all wise and impartial critics will recognize what rank Mas'úd's poems of captivity[1] hold in lofty feeling, and what degree in eloquence. Sometimes, when I read his verses, the hair stands on end on my body, and the tears are like to trickle from my eyes. But when these verses were read to the King, and he heard them, they affected him not at all, and not one particle of his being was warmed to enthusiasm, so that he departed from this world leaving that noble man in prison. Khwája Salmán says:—[2]

مقصور شد مصالح کار جهانیان '
بر حبس و بند این تن رنجور ناتوان '
بر حبس و بند نیز ندارندم استوار '
تا گرد من ندارند ده تن نگاهبان '
هر ده نشسته بر در و در بام سجن من '
با یکدگر دمادم بگویند هر زمان '
هان بر جهید زود که حیلتگریست او '
کز آفتاب پل کند از سایه نردبان '

[1] I adopt B.'s reading, حبستات. A. has حبسیات; L. جلیات.
[2] These verses are inserted in the margin of A. (f. 20v) only.

کمرم کـه سـاختـه شـوم از بهر کارزار
بیرون جهم ز گوشهٔ این سجن ناگهان
با چند کس بر آیم در قلعه گرچه من
شیری شوم معربد و پیلی شوم دمان
پس بی سلاح جنگ چگونه کنم مگر
من سینه‌را سپر کنم و پشت‌را کمان

"Naught served the ends of statesmen save that I,
A helpless exile, should in fetters lie,
Nor do they deem me safe within their cells,
Unless surrounded by ten sentinels;
Which ten sit ever by the gates and walls,
And ever one unto his comrade calls:
'Ho there! On guard! This cunning rogue is one
To fashion bridge and steps from shade and sun!'
Why, grant I stood arrayed for such a fight,
And suddenly sprang forth, attempting flight,
Could elephant or raging lion hope,
Thus cramped in prison-cage, with ten to cope?
Can I, bereft of weapons, take the field,
Or make of back and bosom bow and shield?"

So, by reason of his relation to Sayfu'd-Dawla, he remained imprisoned for twelve years in the days of Sulṭán Ibráhím. And Abú Naṣr of Párs,[1] on account of his like relation, was imprisoned for eight years, though none hath been heard of who hath produced so many splendid elegies and rare gems of verse as were born of his brilliant genius. After eight[2] years Ṭáhir 'Alí of Múshkán, Thiqatu'l-Mulk,

[1] I can find no mention of a poet of this name, and am inclined to think that the author of the oldest extant Persian version of *Kalíla and Dimna* (lithographed at Tabríz, A.H. 1305) is meant. In this volume his name is given as Niḍhámu'd-Dín Abu'l-Ma'álí Naṣru'lláh b. 'Abdu'l-Ḥamíd, but in *M.F.* (vol. i, p. 655) as Naṣíru'd-Dín [b.] 'Abdu'l-Ḥamíd-i-Fársí-i-Shírází. Some of the verses which he composed in prison are there cited.

[2] L. has 'twenty.'

brought him forth from his bondage, so that, in short, during this King's reign that illustrious man spent all his life in captivity, and the ill repute of this deed remained on this House. I hesitate as to the motives which are to be assigned to this act, and whether it is to be ascribed to strength of purpose, or a heedless nature, or hardness of heart, or a malicious disposition. In any case it was not a laudable deed, and I have never met with any sensible man who was prepared to praise that dynasty for such inflexibility of purpose or excess of caution. And I heard it remarked by the King of the World Ghiyáthu'd-Dín wa'd-Dunyá Muḥammad,[1] the son of Malikshàh, at the Gates of Hamadán, on the occasion of the rebellion of his son-in-law, Amír Shihábu'd-Dín Qutulmush Alp Ghází: "It is the sign of a malicious heart to keep a foe imprisoned, for one of two things, either he means well or ill. Then, if the former, it is an injustice to keep him in prison; and if the latter, it is again an injustice to suffer an ill-doer to live." In short that misery of Mas'úd passed, while this ill repute will endure till the Resurrection.

Anecdote xix.

In the time of Sulṭán Khiḍr b. Ibráhím the power of the Kháqánís[2] was at its most flourishing period, while the strength of their administration and the respect in which it was held were such as could not be surpassed.

Now he was a wise, just, and sagacious ruler, and to him appertained the dominion of Transoxania and Turkistán, while he enjoyed the most complete security on the side of Khurásán, wherewith he was allied by friendly relations, kinship, and firm treaties and covenants. And of the

[1] The seventh Seljúq king, who reigned A.H. 498–511 (A.D. 1104–1117).

[2] The dynasty called Ílak Kháns (see Lane's *Muhammadan Dynasties*, pp. 131-135) seems to be meant. L. has '*Sámánís*.' Khiḍr Khán b. Abu'l-Muẓaffar 'Imádu'd-Dawla Ibráhím Tafghách Khán reigned about A.H. 472–488 (A.D. 1079–1095).

splendour maintained by him one detail was this, that when he rode out they carried before his horse, besides other arms, seven hundred maces of gold and silver. He was, moreover, a great patron of poets, and in his service were Amír 'Am'aq,[1] Master Rashídí,[2] Najjár-i-Ságharchí, 'Alí Pánídí,[3] the son of Darghúsh,[4] the son of Isfaráyíní, 'Alí Sipihrí,[5] and Najíbí of Farghána, all of whom obtained rich rewards and vast honours. The Poet-laureate was Amír 'Am'aq, who had profited abundantly by that dynasty and obtained the most ample circumstance, comprising fair damsels, well-paced horses, golden vessels, sumptuous apparel, and servants, biped and quadruped, innumerable. He was greatly honoured at the King's Court, so that of necessity the other poets must needs do him reverence. Such homage as from the others he desired from Master Rashídí also, but herein he was disappointed, for Rashídí, though still young, was nevertheless learned in his art. The Lady Zaynab was the special object of his panegyrics, and he enjoyed the fullest favour of the King, who was continually praising him and asserting his merits, so that Rashídí's affairs prospered, the title of "Prince of poets"[6] was conferred on him, he continued to rise higher in the King's opinion, and from him received gifts of great value.

One day, in Rashídí's absence, the King asked 'Am'aq: "What thinkest thou of the verse of Rashídí, 'the Prince of poets'?" "His verse," replied he, "is extremely good and chaste and correct, but it wants spice."

After some while had elapsed, Rashídí came in and did obeisance, and was about to sit down when the King called him before himself, and said, teasing him as is the way of kings: "I asked the Poet-laureate just now, 'How is Rashídí's poetry?' He replied that it was good, but wanted spice. Now you must compose a quatrain on this

[1] See n. 19 on p. 46 *supra*.
[2] Mentioned briefly in the *Átashkada* amongst the poets of Máwará'u'n-Nahr.
[3] See n. 22 on p. 46 *supra*.
[4] See n. 23 on p. 46 *supra*.
[5] See n. 1 on p. 47 *supra*.
[6] Sayyidu'sh-Shu'ará.

subject." Rashídí, with a bow, sat down in his place and improvised the following fragment:—

شعرهای مرا به بینمکی ' عیب کردی روا بود شاید '
شعر من همچو شکر و شهدست ' واندرین دو نمک نکو نآید '
شلغم و باقلاست گفتهٔ تو ' نمک ای قلتبان ترا باید '

"You stigmatize my verse as 'wanting spice,'
And possibly, my friend, you may be right.
My verse is honey-flavoured, sugar-sweet,
And spice with such could scarcely cause delight.
Spice is for you, you blackguard, not for me,
For beans and turnips is the stuff you write!"

When he recited these verses the King was mightily pleased. And in Transoxania it is the custom and practice to place in the audience-chambers of kings and others gold and silver in trays which they call *sím-ṭáqá* or *juft*;[1] and in this audience of Khiḍr Khán's there were set four trays of red gold, each containing two hundred and fifty dínárs; and these he used to dispense by the handful. On this day he ordered Rashídí to receive all four trays, so he obtained the highest honour, and became famous. For just as a patron becomes famous by the verse of a good poet, so do poets likewise achieve renown by receiving a great reward from the king, these two things being interdependent.

Anecdote xx.

Master Abu'l-Qásim Firdawsí[2] was one of the Dihqáns of Ṭús, from a village called Bázh, in the district of

[1] A. سم طاقا یا . . ; B. سیم طاق یا . . ; L. سم طاق و . . .

[2] This anecdote is cited by Ibn Isfandiyár in his *History of Ṭabaristán* (A.H. 613, A.D. 1216: see Rieu's *Persian Catalogue*, pp. 202–204 and 533b), whence it was excerpted and published, with a German translation, by Ethé (*Z.D.M.G.*, vol. xlviii, pp. 89–94). It was also utilized by Noeldeke in his *Iranische Nationalepos* (*Grundriss d. Iran. Philologie*, vol. ii, p. 130 et seqq.).

Ṭabarán,[1] a large village capable of supplying a thousand men. There Firdawsí enjoyed an excellent position, so that he was rendered quite independent of his neighbours by the income which he derived from his lands, and he had but one child, a daughter. His one desire in putting the Book of Kings (*Sháhnáma*) into verse was, out of the reward which he might obtain for it, to supply her with an adequate dowry. And to this end he left nothing undone, raising his verse as high as heaven, and causing it in sweet fluency to resemble running water. What genius, indeed, could raise verse to such a height as he does in the letter written by Zál to Sám the son of Narímán in Mázandarán, when he desired to ally himself with Rúdába the daughter of the King of Kábul:—[2]

یکی نامه فرمود نزدیک سام   سراسر درود و نوید و سلام
نخست از جهان آفرین یاد کرد   که هم داد فرمود و هم داد کرد
وزو باد بر سام نیرم درود   خداوند شمشیر و گوپال و خود
چمانندهٔ چرمه هنگام کرد   چرانندهٔ کرگس اندر نبرد
فزایندهٔ باد آوردگاه   فشانندهٔ خون ز ابر سیاه
بمردی هنر در هنر ساخته   هنرش از هنر گردن افراخته

"Then to Sám straightway sent he a letter,
Filled with fair praises, prayers, and good greeting.
First made he mention of the World-Maker,
Who doom dispenseth and doom fulfilleth.
'On Nírám's son Sám,' wrote he, 'the sword-lord,
Mail-clad and mace-girt, may the Lord's peace rest!
Hurler of horse troops in hot-contested fights,
Feeder of carrion-fowls with foemen's flesh-feast,

[1] A., B., L. all have "Ṭabaristán." See, however, Noeldeke, loc. cit., p. 161.
[2] These verses (with some variants) will be found on pp. 124–5 of vol. i of Turner Macan's edition of the *Sháhnáma* (Calcutta, 1829).

Raising the roar of strife on the red war-field,
From the grim war-clouds grinding the gore-shower.
Who, by his manly might merit on merit
Heaps, till his merit merit outmeasures.'" [1]

In eloquence I know of no poetry in Persian which equals this, and but little even in Arabic.

When Firdawsí had completed the *Sháhnáma*, it was transcribed by 'Alí Daylam [2] and recited by Abú Dulaf,[2] both of whom he mentions by name in tendering his thanks to Ḥa'íy-i-Quṭayba,[3] the governor of Ṭús, who had conferred on Firdawsí many favours:—

ازین نامه از نامداران شهر ، علی دیلم و بو دلف راست بهر ،
نیامد جز احسنتشان بهره‌ام ، بکفت اندر احسنتشان زهره‌ام ،
حیّیِ قتیبه است از آزادگان ، که از من نخواهد سخن رایگان ،
نیم آگه از اصل و فرع خراج ، همی غلطم اندر میان دواج ،

"*Of the men of renown of this city 'Alí Daylam and Abú Dulaf have participated in this book.*
From them my portion was naught save 'Well done!'
My gall-bladder was like to burst with their 'Well dones.' [4]
Ḥa'íy the son of Quṭayba is a nobleman who asks me not for unrewarded verse.
I am cognizant neither of the principles nor the applications of tax-collecting;
I lounge [at ease] in the midst of my quilt." [5]

[1] Poor as this rendering is, I am strongly of opinion that for an English rendering of the *Sháhnáma* (which always seems to me very analogous in aim, scope, and treatment to that little-read English epic, the Brut of Layamon), the old English alliterative verse would be the most suitable form.

[2] See Noeldeke, loc. cit., p. 153, und n. 2 *ad calc.*

[3] So A. and L. B. has the more usual "Ḥusayn b. Quṭayb." Cf. Noeldeke, loc. cit.

[4] i.e., I am sick of their barren and unprofitable plaudits. As these poor men rendered him material service in other ways, Firdawsí's remarks seem rather ungrateful.

[5] What follows is evidently an explanation of this couplet. Firdawsí means that being no longer vexed with the exactions of the tax-gatherer, he can now repose in peace.

Ḥuyayy the son of Qutayba was the revenue-collector of Ṭús, and deemed it his duty at least to abate the taxes payable by Firdawsí; hence naturally his name will endure till the Resurrection and kings will read it.

So 'Alí Daylam transcribed the *Sháhnáma* in seven volumes, and Firdawsí, taking with him Abú Dulaf, set out for Ghazna. There, by the help of the great Minister Aḥmad Ḥasan[1] the secretary, he presented it, and it was accepted, Sulṭán Maḥmúd expressing himself as greatly indebted to his Minister. But the Prime Minister had enemies who were continually casting the dust of perturbation into the cup of his position, and Maḥmúd consulted with them as to what he should give Firdawsí. They replied: "Fifty thousand dirhams, and even that is too much, seeing that he is in belief a Ráfiḍí and a Mu'tazilite. Of his Mu'tazilite views this verse is a proof:—

به بینندگان آفریننده‌را ' نبینی مرنجان دو بیننده‌را '

' Thy gaze the Creator can never descry;
Then wherefore, by gazing, dost weary thine eye?'

"while to his Ráfiḍí proclivities these verses of his witness:

خداوند[2] گیتی چو دریا نهاد ' بر انگیخته موج از آن تند باد '
چو هفتاد کشتی دران ساخته ' همه بادبانها برافراخته '
میانه یکی خوب کشتی عروس ' بر آراسته همچو چشم خروس '
پیمبر بدو اندران با علی ' همه اهل بیت نبی و ولی '
اگر خلد خواهی بدیگر سرای ' بنزد نبیّ و وصی گیر جای '
گرت زین بد آید گناه منست ' چنین دان و این راه راه منست '
برین زادم و هم برین بگذرم ' یقین دان که خاک پی حیدرم '

[1] So A., B., and L. Noeldeke (loc. cit., p. 163) has Ḥusayn b. Aḥmad.
[2] Both MSS. have خردمند.

'*When the Lord of the World established the Sea, the fierce wind stirred up waves thereon,*
Thereon, as it were, seventy ships wrought, all with sails set.
Amongst them one vessel, fair as a bride, decked with colour like the eye of the cock,
Therein the Prophet with 'Alí, and all the household of the Prophet and his Vicar.
If thou desirest Paradise in the other World, take thy place by the Prophet and his Trustee.
If ill accrues to thee thereby, it is my fault: know this, that this way is my way.
In this I was born, and in this I will pass away: know for a surety that I am as dust at the feet of 'Alí.' "

Now Sulṭán Maḥmúd was a zealot, and he listened to these imputations and caught hold of them, and, to be brief, only twenty[1] thousand dirhams were paid to Ḥakím Firdawsí. He was bitterly disappointed, went to the bath, and, on coming out, bought a drink of sherbet,[2] and divided the money between the bath-man and the sherbet-seller. Knowing, however, Maḥmúd's severity, he fled from Ghazna, and alighted in Herát at the shop of Azraqí's father, Isma'íl the bookseller (*Warráq*), where he remained in hiding for six months, until Maḥmúd's messengers had reached Ṭús and had turned back thence, when Firdawsí, feeling secure, set out from Herát for Ṭús, taking the *Sháhnáma* with him. Thence he came to Ṭabaristán to the Sipahbad Shír-zád of the House of Bávand, who was king there; and this is a noble house which traces its descent from Yazdigird the son of Shahriyár.

Then Firdawsí wrote a satire on Sulṭán Maḥmúd in the Preface, and read a hundred couplets to Shír-zád,[3] saying: "I will dedicate this *Sháhnáma* to you instead of to Sulṭán Maḥmúd, for this book deals wholly with the legends and deeds of thy forebears." Shír-zád treated him with honour

[1] So A. and B., but L. has "sixty thousand."
[2] *Fuqá'*, described as a kind of beer.
[3] Cf. Noeldeke, loc. cit., p. 156, and n. 4 *ad calc.*, where this ruler's name is given as the Ispahbad Shahriyár b. Sharwín.

and showed him many kindnesses, and said: "Maḥmúd was induced to act thus by others, who did not submit your book to him under proper conditions, and misrepresented you. Moreover, you are a Shí'ite, and to one who loves the Family of the Prophet nothing will happen which did not happen to them. Maḥmúd is my liege-lord: let the *Sháhnáma* stand in his name, and give me the satire which you have written on him, that I may expunge it and give you some little recompense; and Maḥmúd will surely summon thee and seek to satisfy thee fully. Do not, then, throw away the labour spent on such a book." And next day he sent Firdawsí 100,000 dirhams, saying: "I buy each couplet at a thousand dirhams; give me those hundred couplets, and rest satisfied therewith." So Firdawsí sent him these verses, and he ordered them to be expunged; and Firdawsí also destroyed his rough copy of them, so that this satire was done away with, and only these few verses remained:—[1]

مرا غمزه کردند کآن پر سخن ، بمهر نبیّ و علی شد کهن ،
اگر مهرشان من حکایت کنم ، چو محمودرا صد حمایت کنم ،
پرستار زاده نیاید بکار ، وگرچند باشد پدر شهریار[2] ،
به نیکی نبد شاه‌را دستگاه ، وگرنه مرا بر نشاندی بگاه ،
چو اندر تبارش بزرگی نبود ، ندانست نام بزرگان شنود ،

"They cast imputations on me, saying: 'That man of many words
Hath grown old in the love of the Prophet and 'Alí.'
If I speak of my love for these
I can protect a hundred such as Maḥmúd.

[1] This is a remarkable statement, and, if true, would involve the assumption that the well-known satire, as we have it, is spurious. Cf. Noeldeke (loc. cit.), pp. 155–156, and n. 1 on the latter.

[2] A. adds another couplet here as follows:—

ازین در سخن چند رانم همی ، چو دریا کرانه ندانم همی ،

No good can come of the son of a slave,
Even though his father hath ruled as King.
The King had no aptitude for good,
Else would he have seated me on a throne.
Since in his family there was no nobility
He could not bear to hear the names of the noble."

In truth good service was rendered to Maḥmúd by Shír-zád, and Maḥmúd was greatly indebted to him.

When I was at Nishápúr in the year A.H. 514 (A.D. 1120–1121), I heard Amír Mu'izzí say that he had heard Amír 'Abdu'r-Razzáq at Ṭús relate as follows:—"Maḥmúd was once in India, and was returning thence towards Ghazna. On the way, as it chanced, there was a rebellious chief possessed of a strong fortress, and next day Maḥmúd encamped at the gates of it, and sent an ambassador to him, bidding him come before him on the morrow, do homage, pay his respects at the Court, receive a robe of honour and return to his place. Next day Maḥmúd rode out with the Prime Minister on his right hand, for the ambassador had turned back and was coming to meet the king. 'I wonder,' said the latter to the Minister, 'what answer he will have given?' The Minister replied:

' اگر جز بکام من آید جواب ' من و گرز و میدان افراسیاب '

' Should the answer come contrary to my wish,
Then for me the mace and the arena of [combat with]
Afrásiyáb.'

'Whose verse,' enquired Maḥmúd, 'is that? For he must have the heart of a man.' 'Poor Abu'l-Qásim Firdawsí composed it,' answered the Minister; 'he who laboured for five and twenty years to complete such a work, and reaped from it no advantage.' 'You speak well,' said Maḥmúd; 'I deeply regret that this noble man was disappointed by me. Remind me at Ghazna to send him something.'

"So when the Sultan returned to Ghazna, the Minister reminded him; and Maḥmúd ordered Firdawsí to be given sixty thousand dínárs' worth of indigo, and that this indigo should be carried to Ṭús on the King's own camels, and that apologies should be made to Firdawsí. For years the Minister had been working for this, and at length he had achieved his work; so now he caused the camels to be loaded, and the indigo arrived safely at Ṭabarán.[1] But as the camels were entering through the Rúdbár Gate, the corpse of Firdawsí was being borne forth from the Gate of Razán.[2] Now at this time there was in Ṭabarán a preacher whose fanaticism was such that he declared that he would not suffer Firdawsí's body to be buried in the Musulmán Cemetery, because he was a Ráfiḍí; and nothing that men could say served to move this doctor. Now outside the gate there was a garden belonging to Firdawsí, and there they buried him, and there he lies to this day." And in the year A.H. 510 (A.D. 1116–1117) I visited his tomb.[3]

They say that Firdowsí left a daughter, of very lofty spirit, to whom they would have given the King's gift; but she would not accept it, saying, "I need it not." The Post-master wrote to the Court and represented this to the King, who ordered that doctor to be expelled from Ṭabarán as a punishment for his officiousness, and to be exiled from his home, and the money to be given to the Imám Abú Bakr Isḥáq for the repair of the rest-house of Chába,[4] which stands on the road between Merv and Níshápúr on the boundaries of Ṭús. When this order reached Ṭús and Níshápúr, it was faithfully carried out; and the restoration of the rest-house of Cháha was effected by this money.

[1] Ṭabarán is the name of a portion of the city of Ṭús. See B. de Meynard's *Dict. de la Perse*, pp. 374–375.

[2] Noeldeke (loc. cit., p. 167, and n. 2 *ad calc.*) has *Razáq* for *Razán*, but A., B., and L. all agree in the latter reading. There are several places called *Rúdbár*, of which one situated near Ṭabarán is probably meant. See B. de Meynard's *Dict. de la Perse*, p. 266. A *Razán* in Sístán is mentioned by *Baládhurí* (pp. 396–397), and another (رزان) in the district of Nasá in Khurásán. (*Dict. de la Perse*, p. 250.)

[3] I am not sure at what point the inverted commas should be inserted, but the last sentence of this paragraph is certainly Niẓámí's.

[4] So B. and L. A. has *Jáha*.

Anecdote xxi.

At the period when I was in the service of that martyred prince the King of the Mountains (may God illuminate his tomb and exalt his station in Paradise!), that august personage had a high opinion of me, and showed himself a most generous patron towards me. Now on the Festival of the Breaking of the Fast one of the nobles of the city of Balkh (may God maintain its prosperity!), Amír 'Amíd Ṣafiyyu'd-Dín Abú Bakr[1] Muḥammad b. al-Ḥusayn Rawánsháhí, came to the Court. He was a young man, an expert writer, a qualified Secretary of State, well endowed with culture and its fruits, popular with all, whose praises were on all tongues. And at this time I was not in attendance.

Now at a reception the King chanced to say, "Call Niḏhámí." Said the Amír 'Amíd Ṣafiyyu'd-Dín, "Is Niḏhámí here?" They answered "Yes." But he supposed that it was Niḏhámí-i-Munírí.[2] "Ah," said he, "a fine poet and a man of wide fame!" When the messenger arrived to summon me, I put on my shoes, and, as I entered, did obeisance, and sat down in my place. When the wine had gone round several times, Amír 'Amíd said, "Niḏhámí has not come." "He is come," replied the King; "see, there he is, seated in such-and-such a place." "I am not speaking of this Niḏhámí," answered Amír 'Amíd; "that Niḏhámí of whom I speak is another one, and as for this one, I do not even know him." Thereupon I saw that the King was vexed; he at once turned to me and said, "Is there another Niḏhámí besides thee?" "Yes, sire," I answered, "there are two other Niḏhámís, one of Samarqand, whom they call Niḏhámí-i-Munírí, and one of Níshápúr, whom they call Niḏhámí-i-Athírí; while me they call Niḏhámí-i-'Arúḍí." "Art thou better, or they?" demanded he. Then Amír 'Amíd perceived that

[1] L. adds 'Ibn'
[2] The reading of this *nisba* is very doubtful in all three texts, both here and lower. In some it appears to read *Minbarí*.

he had spoken ill, and that the King was annoyed. "Sire," said he, "those two Nidhámís are quarrelsome fellows, apt to break up social gatherings by their quarrelsomeness, and to cause trouble, and to do mischief." "Wait," said the King jestingly, "till you see this one drain a bumper and break up the meeting:[1] but of these three Nidhámís which is the best poet?" "Of those two," said the Amír 'Amíd, "I have personal knowledge, having seen them, while this one I have not previously seen, nor have I heard his poetry. If he will compose a couple of verses on this subject which we have been discussing, so that I may see his talents and hear his verse, I will tell you which of these three is best."

Then the King turned to me, saying: "Now, O Nidhámí, do not shame us: say what 'Amíd desires."

Now at that time, when I was in the service of this King, I possessed a copious talent and a brilliant genius, and the favours and gifts of my master had stimulated me to such a point that my improvisations came fluent as running water; so I took up a pen, and, ere the wine-cup had gone twice round, composed these five couplets and submitted them to the King:—

در جهان سه نظامییم ای شاه ' که جهانی ز ما بافغانند '
من بورسا به پیش تخت شهم ' و آن دو در مرو پیش سلطانند '
بحقیقت که در سخن امروز ' هریکی مفخر خراسانند '
گرچه همچون روان سخن گویند ' ورچه همچون خرد سخن دانند '
من شرابم که شان چو در یابم ' هردو از کار خود فرو مانند '

[1] L., which I follow, has: '.. که قدحی بخورد و مجلس‌را برهم زند A. has: .. که پنج قدح سنگی بخورد .. B. has: .. بیقدح سنگی بخورد ..

"*We are three Nidhámis in the world, O King, on account*
of whom a whole world is filled with outcry.
I am at Warsá before the King's throne, while those two
others are in Merv before the Sultan.
To-day, in truth, in verse each one is the Pride of Khurásán.
Although they utter verse subtle as spirit, and although they
understand the Art of Speech like Wisdom,
I am the Wine, for, when I get hold of them, both desist
from their work."

When I submitted these verses, the Amír 'Amíd Ṣafiyyu'd-Dín bowed and said: "O King, let alone the Nidhámís, I know of no poet in all Transoxania, 'Iráq, or Khurásán capable of improvising five such verses, more especially in respect of strength, energy, and sweetness, conjoined with such grace of diction and filled with ideas so original. Rejoice, O Nidhámi, for thou hast no peer on the face of the earth. O sire, he hath a graceful wit, a mind swift to apprehend, and a finished art. By the good fortune of the King of the age and his generosity he hath developed into a unique genius, and will even become more than this, for he is young and hath many days before him."

Thereat the countenance of my King and Lord brightened mightily, and a great cheerfulness appeared in his gracious temperament, and he applauded me, saying: "I give thee the lead-mine of Warsá from this Festival until the Festival of the Sheep-sacrifice. Send an agent there." I did so, sending Isḥáq the Jew. It was the middle of summer, and while they were working it they melted much of the ore, so that in seventy days twelve thousand maunds of lead[1] accrued to me, while the King's opinion of me was increased a thousand-fold. May God (blessed and exalted is He) illuminate his august ashes with the light of His approval,[2] by His Favour and Grace!

[1] A., B. here add: ' از آن خمس.

[2] A. adds after كناد:— و جان شريف اورا بجميع غنا مسرور بمنه آلخ

THIRD DISCOURSE.

On the Nature of the Lore of the Stars, and on the Expert Astrologer.

Abú Rayḥán Bírúní says in the first chapter of his "Explanation of the Science of Astrology" (*Kitábu'l-Tafhím fí ṣaná'ati 't-tanjím*[1]): "A man does not deserve the title of Astrologer until he attains proficiency in four sciences: *first*, Mathematics; *secondly*, Arithmetic; *thirdly*, Cosmography; and *fourthly*, Judicial Astrology."

Now *Mathematical Science* is that whereby are known the natures and qualities of lines and geometrical figures, plain and solid, and the general relations of quantities, and what partakes of the quantitative nature, to what has position and form. It includes the principles of the Book of Euclid the geometrician[2] in the recension of Thábit ibn Qurra.[3]

Arithmetic is that science whereby are known the natures of all sorts of numbers;[4] the nature of their relation to one another; their generation from each other; and the applications thereof, such as halving, doubling, multiplication, division, addition, subtraction, and Algebra. The principles thereof are contained in the book of the 'Αριθμητική, and the applications in the "Supplement" (*Takmila*) of Abú Manṣúr of Baghdad,[5] and the "Hundred Chapters" (*Ṣad Báb*) of as-Sajzí.[6]

[1] See Rieu's *Persian Catalogue*, pp. 451–2, where a MS. of the Persian version of this work, dated A.H. 685 (A.D. 1286), is described.

[2] I suppose that this is the meaning of مجّار in the text.

[3] I take this to be the sense of L.'s reading: که ثابت بن قرّه دستی کرده است. For دستی A. appears to read وستی, and B. دسبی. Concerning Thábit b. Qurra, see Wüstenfeld's *Gesch. d. Arabischen Aerzte*, pp. 34–36, Brockelmann's *Gesch. d. Arab. Litteratur*, pp. 217, 218, etc. He was born in A.H. 221 (A.D. 836) and died A.H. 288 (A.D. 901).

[4] A. adds و خاصّه هر نوعی از در نفس خویش.

[5] Abú Manṣúr 'Abdu'l-Qáhir b. Ṭáhir al-Baghdádí, d. A.H. 429 (A.D. 1037). See Ḥájjí Khalífa, No. 3,253.

[6] Abú Sa'íd Aḥmad b. Muḥammad b. 'Abdu'l-Jalíl as-Sajzí (or Sijzí, i.e. of Sajistán or Sístán). See Brockelmann, op. cit., p. 219.

Cosmography is that science whereby are known the natures of the Celestial and Terrestrial Bodies,[1] their shapes and positions, their relations to one another, and the measurements and distances which are between them, together with the nature of the movements of each one of the stars and heavens, and the co-ordination of the spheres, axes, and circles whereby these movements are fulfilled. It includes a knowledge of the Al-Magest and the best of its commentaries and elucidations, which are the Commentary of Tabrízí[2] and the Al-Magest of Shifá. And amongst the applications of this science is the science of the Calendar and of Almanacs.

Judicial Astrology is a branch of Natural Science, and its special use is prognostication, by which is meant the deducing by analogy from configurations, and from an estimation of the degrees and zodiacal signs and their influences, those events which are brought about by their movements, in respect to the condition of the cycles of the world, politics, cities, nativities, changes, transitions, decisions, and other questions; and it is contained in these five [books] which we have enumerated, to wit, the writings of Abú Ma'shar of Balkh,[3] Aḥmad 'Abdu'l-Jalíl-i-Sajzí, Abú Rayḥán Bírúní, and Gúshyár-i-Jílí.[4]

So the Astrologer must be a man of acute mind, approved character, and great natural intelligence. And one of the essentials of this art is that the astrologer who would pronounce prognostications should possess in his own horoscope the Share of the Unseen, and that the Lord of the House of this Share of the Unseen should be lucky, and in a favourable position, in order that such pronouncements as he gives may be near the truth. And one of the

[1] For أجرام ("bodies") A., B. have اجزاء عالم, "the nature of the constituent parts of the Celestial and Terrestrial Realms."

[2] See the long article on *al-Majistí* in Ḥájí Khalífa (No. 11,413). The *Tabrízí* intended is probably al-Faḍl b. Ḥátim of Tabríz.

[3] See Brockelmann, op. cit., pp. 221, 222.

[4] See ibid., pp. 222, 223. Both forms of the *nisba* (Jílí and Jabalí) are found in the texts.

conditions of being a good astrologer is that he should have in mind the whole of the "Principia" (*Uṣúl*) of Gúshyár, and should continually study the "Opus Majus,"[1] and should look frequently into the *Qánún-i-Mas'údí*[2] and the *Jámi'-i-Sháhí*, so that his knowledge and concepts may be refreshed.

Anecdote xxii.

Ya'qúb b. Isḥáq al-Kindí,[3] though he was a Jew, was the philosopher of his age and the wisest man of his time, and stood high in the service of al-Ma'mún. One day he came in before al-Ma'mún, and sat down above one of the Imáms of Islám. Said this man, "Thou art of a subject race;[4] why, then, dost thou sit above the Imáms of Islám?" "Because," said Ya'qúb, "I know what thou knowest, while thou knowest not what I know."

Now this person knew of his skill in Astrology, but had no knowledge of his other attainments in science. "I will write down," said he, "something on a piece of paper, and if thou canst divine what I have written, I will admit your claim." Then they laid a wager, on the part of this person a cloak, and on the part of Ya'qúb a mule and its trappings, worth a thousand dínárs, which was standing at the door. Then the former asked for an inkstand and paper, wrote something on a piece of paper, placed it under the Caliph's quilt, and cried, "Out with it!" Ya'qúb b. Isḥáq asked for a tray of earth, rose up, took the altitude, ascertained the ascendant, drew an astrological table on the tray of earth, determined the positions of the stars, fixed the signs of the Zodiac, worked out the subjective conditions and

[1] و كار مهتر پيوسته مطالعه مى كند. From the context, some book would seem to be intended.

[2] By Abú Rayḥán al-Bírúní. See *Ḥájí Khalífa*, No. 9,369.

[3] See Wüstenfeld's *Gesch. d. Arab. Aerzte*, pp. 21, 22. He died about A.H. 260 (A.D. 873).

[4] 'تو مرد ذمّى باشى.'

affinities,[1] and said, "On that paper he has written something which was first a plant and then an animal." Al-Ma'mún put his hand under the quilt and drew forth the paper, on which was written "The Rod of Moses." Al-Ma'mún was filled with wonder and expressed his astonishment. Then Ya'qúb took the cloak of his adversary, and cut it in two before al-Ma'mún, saying, "I will make it into two . . . ."[2]

This matter became generally known in Baghdad, whence it spread to 'Iráq and throughout Khurásán, and was widely discussed. A certain doctor of Balkh, prompted by that fanatical zeal which characterizes the learned, obtained a book on Astrology and placed a knife in the middle of it, intending to go to Baghdad, attend the lectures of Ya'qúb b. Isḥáq al-Kindí, make a beginning in Astrology, and, when he should find a suitable opportunity, suddenly kill him. Stage by stage he advanced, until he went in to the hot bath and came out, arrayed himself in clean clothes, and, placing this book in his sleeve, set out for Ya'qúb's house.

When he reached the gate of the house, he saw standing there many handsomely-caparisoned horses belonging to descendants of the Prophet[3] and other eminent and noble persons of Baghdad. Having made enquiries, he went in, entered the circle in front of Ya'qúb, greeted him, and said, "I desire to study somewhat of the science of the stars with our Master." "Thou hast come from the East to slay me on a pretence of studying Astrology," replied Ya'qúb, "but thou wilt repent of thine intention, study the stars, and

[1] Neither the meaning nor the wording of this sentence is clear to me. L. has 'شرایط خبی و صمر بعمل آورد'. For خبی A. and B. have جی or حبی, the reading being uncertain.

[2] Some sort of garment seems to be meant, but neither the reading nor the meaning is clear. L. has 'دو پاره را فتات کنم'; A., 'دو پاقنابه کنم'; B., 'دو بافتابه کنم'.

[3] Literally, "of the Banú Háshim."

attain perfection in that science, and wilt become one of the greatest Astrologers in the Church of Muḥammad (on whom be God's Blessing and Peace)." All the great men there assembled were astonished; and Abú Ma'shar[1] confessed and produced the knife from the middle of the book, broke it, and cast it away. Then he bent his knees and studied for fifteen years, until he reached that eminence which he reached in Astrology.

Anecdote xxiii.

It is stated that once when Sulṭán Maḥmúd b. Náṣiru'd-Dín[2] was sitting on the roof of a four-doored summer-house in Ghazna, in the Garden of a Thousand Trees, he turned his face to Abú Rayḥán[3] and said, "By which of these four doors shall I go out?" (for all four were practicable) "Decide, and write the decision on a piece of paper, and put it under my quilt." Abú Rayḥán called for an astrolabe, took the altitude, worked out the ascendant, reflected for a while, and then wrote down his decision on a piece of paper, and placed it under the quilt. "Hast thou decided?" asked Maḥmúd. He answered, "Yes."

Then Maḥmúd bade them make an opening in the wall, and they brought mattocks and spades, and in the wall which was on the eastern side dug out a fifth door, through which he went out. Then he bade them bring the paper. So they brought it, and on it was written: "He will go out through none of these four doors, but they will dig a fifth door on the side of the eastern wall, by which door he will go forth." Maḥmúd, on reading this, was furious, and bade them cast Abú Rayḥán down from the midst of the palace. So they did even as he had said. Now

[1] See Brockelmann's *Gesch. d. Arab. Litteratur*, pp. 221, 222.
[2] i.e. the great Sulṭán Maḥmúd of Ghazna (reigned A.H. 388-421, A.D. 998-1030).
[3] i.e. the celebrated al-Bírúní, of whom mention has been already made.

a net had been stretched here to keep off the flies,[1] and on it Abú Rayḥán fell. The net tore, and he subsided gently to the ground, so that he received no injury. "Bring him in," said Maḥmúd. So they brought him in, and Maḥmúd said: "O Abú Rayḥán, didst thou know this?" "I know it, sire," he answered, and, taking the Almanac from the servant, produced the prognostications out of the Almanac;[2] and amongst the predictions for that day was written: "To-day they will cast me down from a high place, but I shall reach the earth in safety, and arise sound in body."

All this was not according to Maḥmúd's mind. He waxed still angrier, and ordered Abú Rayḥán to be detained in the citadel. So Abú Rayḥán was confined in the citadel of Ghazna, where he remained for six months. It is said that during that period of six months none dared speak to Maḥmúd about Abú Rayḥán, one of whose servants was, however, deputed to wait upon him, and to go out to get what he wanted, and to return therewith. One day this servant was passing through the Park of Ghazna,[3] when a fortune-teller called to him and said, "I perceive several things worth mentioning in your fortune: give me a present, that I may reveal them to you." The servant gave him two dirhams, whereupon the soothsayer said: "One dear to thee is in affliction, but ere three days are past he will be delivered from that affliction, will be invested with a robe of honour, and will again be loaded with honours and favours."

The servant proceeded to the citadel, and told this incident to his master as a piece of good tidings. Abú

[1] This seems to be the meaning of L.'s reading: مگر راد مگس‌را دامی بسته بودند. A. and B. are illegible. The former seems to have, مگر تا سام سانکش‌را; the latter, مگر با شام مسانکس‌را دامی .. وامی ..

[2] و تحویل از میان تقویم بیرون کرد

[3] بسر مرغزار غزنین ..

Rayḥán smiled and said, "O foolish fellow, dost thou not know that on such occasions one ought not to stand still? Thou hast informed me too late."[1] It is said that the Prime Minister Aḥmad Ḥasan of Maymand (may God be merciful to him!) was for six months seeking an opportunity to say a word on behalf of Abú Rayḥán. At length, when engaged in the chase, he found the King in a good humour, and, working from one topic to another, he brought the conversation round to Astrology. Then he said: "Poor Abú Rayḥán uttered two such good prognostications, and instead of decorations and a robe of honour obtained bonds and imprisonment." "Know, my lord," replied Maḥmúd, "for I have proved it,[2] that this man is said to have no equal in the world save Abú 'Alí Síná (Avicenna), but both his prognostications were opposed to my will; and kings are like little children[3]—in order to receive rewards from them, one should speak in accordance with their opinion. It would have been better for him on that day if one of those two prognostications had been wrong. But to-morrow order him to be brought forth, and to be given a horse caparisoned with gold, a royal robe, a satin turban, a thousand dínárs, a slave, and a handmaiden."

So, on the very day specified by the soothsayer, they brought forth Abú Rayḥán, and the gift of honour detailed above was conferred upon him, and the King apologized to him, saying: "If thou desirest always to reap advantage from me, speak according to my desire, not according to the dictates of thy science." So thereafter Abú Rayḥán altered his practice; and this is one of the conditions of the service of kings, that one must be with them in right or wrong, and speak according to their wish.

Now when Abú Rayḥán reached his house, the learned

[1] Instead of this sentence A. has: "Thou hast wasted two dirhams."

[2] I follow L., which reads: ‹بدان ای خواجه و من یافته ام›. A. has: ‹خواجه بدان که من ندانسته ام›

[3] A. omits this simile.

came to congratulate him. He related to them the incident of the soothsayer, whereat they were amazed, and sent to summon him. They found him most illiterate, knowing nothing. Then Abú Rayḥán said, "Hast thou the horoscope of thy nativity?" "I have," replied he. Then Abú Rayḥán examined it, and the Share of the Unseen fell directly on the degree of his Ascendant,[1] so that whatever he said, though he spoke blindly, came near to the truth.

Anecdote xxiv.

I had in my employment a woman-servant, who was born on the 28th of Ṣafar, A.H. 510[2] (=July 12th, A.D. 1116), when the Moon was in conjunction with the Sun and there was no distance between them, so that both the Share of Fortune and the Share of the Unseen fell on the degree of the Ascendant. When she reached the age of fifteen years, I taught her Astrology, in which she became so skilful that she could answer difficult questions in this science, and her prognostications came very near the truth. Ladies used to come to her and question her, and the most part of what she said coincided with the pre-ordained decrees of fate.

One day an old woman came and said: "It is now four years since a son of mine went on a journey, and I have no news of him, neither of his life nor of his death. See whether, wherever he may be, he is of the living or the dead." So the woman-astrologer arose, took the altitude, worked out the degree of the Ascendant, drew out an astrological table, and determined the positions of the stars; and the very first words she said were, "Thy son hath returned!"

The old woman was annoyed and said: "O child, I have no hopes of my son's coming: tell me this much, is he alive or dead?"

[1] سهم الغیبش بر حاقّ درجهٔ طالع افتاده بود . .

[2] A. has "512."

"I tell you," said the other, "thy son hath come. Go, and, if he hath not come, return, that I may tell thee how he is."

So the old woman went to her house, and lo! her son had arrived and was unloading his asses. She embraced him, took off her veil, and came back to the woman-astrologer, saying, "Thou didst speak truly; my son hath come, bringing presents"; and she gave her her blessing. When I came home and heard tidings of this, I enquired of her, "By what didst thou speak, and from what House didst thou deduce this prognostication?" She answered: "I had not reached so far as this. When I had finished the figure of the Ascendant, he came in and sat down on the letter of the degree of the Ascendant, wherefore it so seemed in my mind, that this young man had returned. When I said so, and the mother had gone to find out, it became so certain to me that it was as though I actually saw him unloading his asses."

Then I perceived that it was the Share of the Unseen, and nothing else but this, which thus influenced the degree of the Ascendant.

Anecdote xxv.

Maḥmúd Dá'údí, the son of Abu'l-Qásim Dá'údí, was a great fool, nay, almost a madman, and had no considerable knowledge as to the actions of the stars; yet he could cast a nativity, and in his notebook were figures declaring "it is" or "it is not." He was in the service of Amír Dá'úd Abú Bakr Mas'úd at Panj-dih; and his prognostications generally came right.

Now his madness was such that when my master the King of the Mountains sent him a pair of Ghúrí dogs, very large and formidable, he fought with them of his own free-will, and escaped from them in safety. Years afterwards we were sitting with a number of persons of learning in the Perfumers' Market at Herát, in the shop of Muqrí the surgeon-druggist,[1] and discussing all manner of subjects. One of these learned men happening to remark, "What a great man was Avicenna (Ibn Síná)!" I saw Dá'údí fly into a passion, all the possession of anger appearing in and overcoming him, and he cried: "O so-and-so, who was Abú 'Alí? I regard myself as equal in worth to a thousand Abú 'Alí's, for he never even fought with a cat, whilst I fought before Amír Dá'úd with two dogs." So on that day I knew him to be mad; yet for all his madness I witnessed the following occurrence.

In the year A.H. 505[2] (A.D. 1111–1112), when Sulṭán Sanjar encamped in the Plain of Khúzán,[3] on his way to Transoxania to fight with Muḥammad,[4] Amír Dá'úd attached himself to the King, and made a great entertainment for him. On the third day the King came to the river-brink, and entered a boat to amuse himself with fishing. In the boat he summoned Dá'údí before him to talk after the manner of madmen, while he laughed, for Dá'údí would openly abuse Amír Dá'úd.

Presently the King said to him, "Prognosticate how many maunds the fish which I shall catch this time will weigh." Dá'údí said, "Draw up your hook." So the king drew it up; and he took the altitude, paused for a while, and then said, "Now cast it." The King cast, and he said, "I prognosticate that this fish which you will draw out will weigh five maunds." "O knave," said Amír Dá'úd, "whence should fish of five maunds' weight come into this stream?" "Be silent," said Dá'údi; "what do you know about it?" So Amír Dá'úd was silent, fearing that, should he insist further, he would only get abuse

[1] The readings differ here. L. has . . بدكان مقرى عطّار طبيب .
A., B. have . . بر دكان مقرى حدّاد طبيب .

[2] A. has 508.

[3] See Barbier de Meynard's *Dict. de la Perse*, pp. 215, 216. A. reads *Khúz*, B. *Khúzí*.

[4] Apparently his brother, Ghiyáthu'd-Dín Abú Shujá' Muḥammad the Seljúq is meant. He reigned A.H. 498–511 (A.D. 1104–1117).

Suddenly there was a pull on the line, indicating that a fish had been taken captive. The King drew in the line with a very large fish on it, which, when weighed, scaled five[1] maunds. All were amazed, and expressed their astonishment. "Dá'údí," said the King, "what dost thou wish for?" "O King," said he with an obeisance, "of all that is on this earth I desire but a coat of mail, a shield, and a spear, that I may do battle with Báwardí." And this Abíwardí was the Captain of Amír Dá'úd's gate, and Dá'údí entertained towards him a fanatical hatred, because the title of Shujá'u'l-Mulk had been conferred upon him, while Dá'údí himself bore the title of Shujá'u'l-Ḥukamá, and grudged that the other should be so entitled. And the Amír, well knowing this, used continually to embroil Dá'údí with him, and this good Musulmán was at his wits' end by reason of him.

In short, as to Maḥmúd Dá'údí's madness there was no doubt, and I have mentioned this matter in order that the King may know that folly and insanity are amongst the conditions of this craft.

Anecdote xxvi.

Ḥakím-i-Mawṣilí was one of the order of Astrologers in Níshápúr, and was in the service of that great Minister Nidhámu'l-Mulk of Ṭús, who used to consult with him on matters of importance, and seek his advice and opinion. Now when Mawṣilí's years were drawing to a close, and great decrepitude appeared in him, and feebleness of body began to show itself, so that he was no longer able to perform these long journeys, he asked the Minister's permission to go and reside at Níshápúr, and to send thence annually the almanac and forecast for the year.

Now the Minister Nidhámu'l-Mulk was also in the decline of life and near the term of existence; and he said: "Look

[1] A. has "six."

so much at the lapse of my life as to observe when the dissolution of my elemental nature will occur, and at what epoch that inevitable fate and unavoidable sentence will befal."

Ḥakím-i-Mawṣilí answered, "Six months after my death." So the Minister ordered him to receive all things needful for his comfort, and Mawṣilí went to Níshápúr, and there abode in ease, sending each year the forecast and calendar. And whoever came to the Minister from Níshápúr, he used first to enquire, "How is Mawṣilí?" And so soon as he had news of his safety, he would become joyous and cheerful.

At length, in the year A.H. 485 (= A.D. 1092–3), one arrived from Níshápúr, and the Minister enquired of him concerning Mawṣilí. The man replied, with an obeisance: "May he who holdeth the chief seat in al-Islám be the heir of many lifetimes! Mawṣilí hath quitted this mortal body." "When?" enquired the Minister. "In the middle of Rabí' the First" (April 11–May 11, A.D. 1092), answered the man, "he yielded up his life for him who sitteth in the chief seat of al-Islám."

The Minister thereat was mightily put about, and was warned, and looked into all his affairs, and confirmed all his pious endowments, and gave effect to his bequests,[1] and wrote his last testament, and set free such of his slaves as had earned his approval, and discharged the debts which he owed, and, so far as lay in his power, made all men content with him, and sought forgiveness from his adversaries, and made his will, and so sat awaiting his fate until the month of Ramaḍán (A.H. 485 = Oct. 5–Nov. 4, A.D. 1092), when he fell a martyr at the hands of that Sect (i.e. the Assassins); may God make illustrious his Proof, and accord him an ample Approval!

Since the Ascendant ruling his nativity, the observation, the Lord of the Sign, and the dominant factor were rightly

[1] A., which I follow, has ادرارات را (اوزار را .L) توقیع کرد

determined, and the Astrologer was expert and accomplished, naturally the prognostication came true.[1]

Anecdote xxvii.

In the year A.H. 506 (A.D. 1112–1113) Khwája Imám 'Umar Khayyám[2] and Khwája Imám Mudhaffar-i-Isfizárí had alighted in the city of Balkh, in the street of the Slave-sellers, in the house of Amír Abú Sa'd,[3] and I had joined that assembly. In the midst of our convivial gathering I heard that Argument of Truth (*Ḥujjatu'l-Ḥaqq*) 'Umar say, "My grave will be in a spot where the trees will shed their blossoms on me twice in each year." This thing seemed to me impossible, though I knew that one such as he would not speak idle words.

When I arrived at Níshápúr in the year A.H. 530 (A.D. 1135–6), it being then some years since that great man had veiled his countenance in the dust, and this lower world had been bereaved of him, I went to visit his grave on the eve of a Friday (seeing that he had the claim of a master on me), taking with me a guide to point out to me his tomb. So he brought me out to the Ḥíra[4] Cemetery; I turned to the left, and his tomb lay at the foot of a garden-wall, over which pear-trees and peach-trees thrust their heads, and on his grave had fallen so many flower-leaves that his dust was hidden beneath the flowers. Then I remembered that saying which I had heard from him

[1] I confess that these astrological terms are beyond me. Several of them (e.g. *haylâj* and *kadkhuda*) are explained in the section of the *Mafátíḥu'l-'ulúm* which treats of Astrology (ed. Van Vloten, pp. 226–232). The first part of the sentence runs:

چون طالع مولود و رصد و كدخدا و هيلاج درست بود . . .

[2] A. and B. have *Khayyámí*, the form usually found in Arabic books.

[3] A. adds جرّه, while B. calls him بو سعيد حرّه.

[4] So A., B., and L., but in the margin of the latter is the following gloss:

حيره چو ميرى ايوان و طاق و رواق (برهان)

in the city of Balkh, and I fell to weeping, because on the face of the earth, and in all the regions of the habitable globe, I nowhere saw one like unto him. May God (blessed and exalted is He) have mercy upon him,[1] by His Grace and His Favour! Yet although I witnessed this prognostication on the part of that Proof of the Truth 'Umar, I did not observe that he had any great belief in astrological predictions; nor have I seen or heard of any of the great [scientists] who had such belief.[2]

Anecdote xxviii.

In the winter of the year A.H. 508 (= A.D. 1114–1115) the King sent a messenger to Merv to the Prime Minister Ṣadru'd-Dín Muḥammad b. al-Mudhaffar (on whom be God's Mercy) bidding him tell Khwája Imám 'Umar to select a favourable time for him to go hunting, such that therein should be no snowy or rainy days. For Khwája Imám 'Umar was in the Minister's company, and used to lodge at his house.

So the Minister sent a messenger to summon him, and told him what had happened. The Khwája went and looked into the matter for two days, and made a careful choice; and he himself went and superintended the mounting of the King at the auspicious moment. When the King was mounted and had gone but a short distance,[3] the sky became overcast with clouds, a wind arose, and snow and mist supervened. All present fell to laughing, and the King desired to turn back; but Khwája Imám ['Umar] said: "Have no anxiety, for this very hour the clouds will clear away, and during these five days there will be not a drop of moisture." So the King rode on, and the clouds

[1] A. has: "cause him to dwell in Paradise."

[2] L. omits this last sentence.

[3] I suppose this to be the meaning of the words: و یک بانگ زمین برفت, which is the reading of all three texts.

opened, and during those five days there was no moisture, and no one saw a cloud.

But prognostication by the stars, though a recognized art, is not to be relied on, and whatever the astrologer predicts he must leave to Fate.

Anecdote xxix.

It is incumbent on the King, wherever he goes, to prove such companions and servants as he has with him; and if one is a believer in the Holy Law, and scrupulously observes the rites and duties thereof, he should make him an intimate, and treat him with honour, and confide in him; but if otherwise, he should drive him away, and guard even the outskirts of his environment from his very shadow. Whoever does not believe in the religion and law of Muḥammad the Chosen One, in him can no man trust, and he is unlucky, both to himself and to his master.

In the beginning of the reign of the king Saltán Ghiyáthu'd-Dunyá wa'd-Dín Muḥammad b. Malikshâh, styled Qasímu Amíri'l-Múminín (may God illuminate his proof!),[1] the King of the Arabs, Sadaqa,[2] revolted and withdrew his neck from the yoke of allegiance, and with fifty thousand Arab horsemen marched on Baghdad from Hilla. The Prince of Believers al-Mustadhhbir bi'lláh had sent off letter after letter and courier after courier to Isfahán,[3] summoning the Sultan, who sought from the astrologers the determination of the auspicious moment. But no such determination could be made which would suit the Lord of the King's Ascendant, which was retrograde. So they said, "We find no auspicious moment." "Seek it, then," said he; and he was very urgent in the matter, and much vexed in mind. And so the astrologers fled.

[1] Reigned A.H. 498-511, A.D. 1104–1117.

[2] Cf. Houtsma's ed. of al-Bundárí's *History of the Seljúqs*, p. 185, where an Amír of this name is mentioned under the year A.H. 531.

[3] A. calls it *Sipahán*.

Now there was a stranger of Jayy[1] who had a shop by the Gate of the Dome and who used to take omens; and men and women of every class used to visit him, and he used to write for them amulets and charms, but he had no profound knowledge. By means of an acquaintance with one of the King's servants he brought himself to the King's notice, and said: "I will find an auspicious moment: depart in that, and if thou dost not return victorious, then cut off my head."

So the King was pleased, and mounted his horse at the moment declared auspicious by him, and gave him two hundred dínárs of Níshápúr, and went forth, fought with Ṣadaqa, defeated his army, took him captive, and put him to death. And when he returned triumphant and victorious to Isfahán, he heaped favours on the soothsayer, ordered him to receive great honours, and made him one of his intimates. Then he summoned the astrologers and said: "You did not find an auspicious moment, it was this stranger of Jayy who found it; and I went, and God justified the omen.[2] Probably Ṣadaqa had sent you a bribe so that you should not name the auspicious time." Then they all fell to the earth, lamenting and exclaiming: "The astrologers were not satisfied with that moment. If you wish, write a message and send it to Khurásán, and see what Khwája Imám 'Umar Khayyám says."

The King saw that the poor wretches did not speak amiss. He therefore summoned one of his courtiers and said: "Invite this stranger of Jayy[3] to your house, drink wine with him, and treat him with kindly familiarity; and, when he is overcome with wine, enquire of him, saying,

[1] A suburb of Isfahán, as is explained in a marginal gloss in L., which has this reading: غریب جی (printed in the text as one word, عریبجی). A. reads غزنوی and B. غرنوی.

[2] A. adds "Wherefore did ye act thus?"

[3] L. is constant in this reading, but here A. has غریبجی را and B. غرانجی را.

'Was that moment determined by thee not good? For the astrologers find fault with it. Tell me the secret of this.'"

Then the courtier did so, and, when his guest was drunk, made this enquiry of him. The soothsayer answered: "I know that one of two things must happen; either that army would be defeated, or this one. If the former, then I should be loaded with honours; and if the latter, how should the King concern himself with me?"

Next day the courtier reported this conversation to the King, who ordered the strange soothsayer to be expelled, because one who held such views about good Musulmáns was unlucky. Then[1] the King summoned his own astrologers and restored his confidence to them, saying: "I know that this soothsayer never said his prayers, and one who agrees not with our Holy Law agrees not with us."

Anecdote XXX.

In the year A.H. 547 (A.D. 1152–3) a battle was fought between that king of blessed memory Sanjar b. Maliksháh and my lord the king 'Alá'u'd-Dín wa'd-Dunyá; and the army of Ghúr was defeated, and my lord the King of the East was taken prisoner, and my lord's son the Just King Shamsu'd-Dawla wa'd-Dín Maḥmúd b. Mas'úd was taken captive at the hands of the Commander-in-chief (*Amír-i-sipahsálár*). The ransom was fixed at fifty thousand dínárs of pure gold,[2] and a messenger from him was to go to the Court at Bámiyán to ask for this sum; and when it should be sent the Prince was to be released, while the King himself was granted his liberty by the Lord of the World (Sanjar), who, moreover, at the time of his departure from

[1] A. adds "they killed him, and . . . ."

[2] The words بر نقش هريوه are omitted in L. For this meaning of هريوه see Vuller's *Persian Lexicon*, s.v.

Herát, granted him a robe of honour; and it was under these circumstances that I arrived to wait upon him.[1]

One day, being extremely sad at heart, he signed to me, and enquired when this deliverance would finally be accomplished, and when this consignment would arrive. So I took an observation that day with a view to making this prognostication, and worked out the ascendant, exerting myself to the utmost, and [ascertained that] there was an indication of a satisfactory solution to the question on the third day. So next day I came and said: "To-morrow at the time of the first prayer the messenger will arrive." All that night the Prince was thinking about this matter. Next day I hastened to wait on him. "To-day," said he, "is the time fixed." "Yes," I replied; and continued with him till the first prayer. When the call to prayer was sounded, he remarked reproachfully: "The first prayer has arrived, but still no news!" Even while he was thus speaking, a courier arrived bringing the good tidings that the consignment had come, consisting of fifty thousand dínárs, sheep, and other things, and that 'Izzu'd-Dín Maḥmúd,[2] the steward of Prince Ḥusámu'd-Dawla wa'd-Dín, was in charge of the convoy. My lord Shamsu'd-Dawla wa'd-Dín was invested with the King's dress of honour, and very shortly regained his beloved home, and from that time his affairs have prospered more and more every day (may they continue so to do!). And thence it was that he used to treat me with the utmost kindness and say: "Nidhámí, do you remember making such a prognostication in Herát, and how it came true? I wanted to fill thy mouth with gold, but there I had no gold, though here

[1] The text is rather obscure here. It runs: وازجانب [جوانب] سلطان عالم او خود مطلق بود بوقت حرکت کردن از هرات تشریف [نامزد] کرده بود و من بنده درین حال بخدمت رسیدم٬

[2] A. adds حاجی.

I have." Then he called for gold, and filled my mouth therewith till it would contain no more, whereupon he said, "Hold out thy sleeve." So I held it out, and he filled it also with gold. May God (blessed and exalted is He) maintain this dynasty in daily-increasing prosperity, and long spare those two Princes to my august Master, by His favour, bounty, and grace! Amen, O Lord of the Worlds!

Fourth Discourse.

On the Nature of the Science of Medicine, and the grades[1] of Physicians.

Medicine is that art whereby the health of the human body is preserved; whereby, when it wanes, it is restored; and whereby the body is embellished by long hair, a clean complexion, freshness and vigour.

Excursus.

The physician should be of tender disposition, of wise and gentle nature, and more especially an acute observer, capable of benefiting everyone by accurate diagnoses, that is to say, by rapid deduction of the unknown from the known. And no physician can be of tender disposition if he fails to recognize the nobility of man; nor of philosophical nature unless he knows Logic, nor an acute observer unless he be strengthened by God's guidance; and he who is not an acute observer will not arrive at a correct understanding of the cause of any ailment, for he must form his opinion from the pulse, which has a systole, a diastole, and a pause between these two movements.

Now here there is a difference of opinion amongst physicians, one school maintaining that it is impossible by palpation to gauge the movement of contraction; but

[1] For مراتب A has هداية.

that most accomplished of the moderns, that talented man Abú 'Alí al-Husayn b. 'Abdu'lláh Síná (Avicenna),[1] says in his book the *Qánún* that the movement of contraction also can be gauged, though with difficulty, in thin subjects;[2] and that the pulse is of two sorts, each of which is divided into three subordinate varieties, namely, its two extremes and its mean; but, unless the Divine guidance assist the physician in his search for the truth, his thought will not hit the mark. So also the examination of the urine, and the observing of its colour and peculiarities, and the deducing somewhat from each colour, is no easy matter; for these deductions are dependent on Divine help and Heavenly guidance; and this is the quality which we have already mentioned under the name of acumen. And unless the physician knows Logic, and understands the meaning of species and genus, he cannot discriminate between that which appertains to the category and that which is peculiar to the individual, and so will not recognize the cause of the disease. And, failing to recognize the cause, he will not succeed in his treatment. But let us now give an illustration, so that it may be known that it is as we say. Disease[3] is the genus; fever, cold, headache, dizziness, scarlet fever, and jaundice are the species, each of which is distinguished from the others by a diagnostic sign, while each itself is again divisible into varieties. For instance, 'Fever' is the genus, wherein quotidian, tertian, double tertian, quartan, and the sub-varieties of each, are distinguished from each other by a special diagnostic sign, so that, for instance, quotidian is distinguished from other

[1] See De Slane's translation of *Ibn Khallikán*, vol. i, pp. 440-446; von Kremer's *Culturgeschichte d. Orients*, vol. ii, pp. 455, 460; Wüstenfeld's *Gesch. d. Arab Aerzte*, pp. 64-75, etc. The *Qánún* was printed at Rome, A.D. 1593.

[2] A. reads:

'حرکت انقباض را در توان یافت بدشواری اندر تنهاء بی گوشت'

This is no doubt the correct reading, not تنهائی گوشت as in B and L.

[3] L. here has محض جنس آمد, instead of the correct reading of A., . . مرض.

fevers by the fact that the longest period thereof is a day and a night, and that in it there is no rigor, heaviness, lassitude, nor pain.[1] Again, inflammatory fever[2] is distinguished from other fevers by this, that when it lays hold of anyone it does not abate for several days; while tertian is distinguished by the fact that it comes one day and not the next; and double tertian by this, that one day it comes with a higher temperature and a shorter interval, and another day in a milder form with a longer interval; while, lastly, quartan is distinguished by this, that for two days it does not come and the third day it comes.

Each of these, again, comprises several varieties, and each of these in turn sundry sub-varieties; and if the physician be versed in Logic and possessed of acumen, he will know which fever it is, what the *materies morbi* is, and whether it is simple or compound, and he can then at once proceed to treat it; but if he fail to recognize the disease, then let him turn to God and seek help from Him; and so likewise, if he fail in his treatment, let him have recourse to God, seeing that the issue is in His hands.

Anecdote xxxi.

In the year A.H. 512,[3] in the Druggists' Bazaar of Níshápúr, at the shop of Muḥammad Ḍakhm the Physician,[4] I heard Khwája Imám Abú Bakr Daqqáq saying: "A certain man of Níshápúr[5] was seized with the colic and called me in. I examined him, and proceeded to treat him,

[1] . و درو تكسّر و گرانى و كاهلى و درد نباشد

[2] تب مطبقه . See Schlimmer's *Terminologie Médico-Pharmaceutique* (lithographed at Ṭihrán, A.H. 1874), pp. 192–197 and 285. Perhaps, however, it should here be translated "remittent."

[3] A. has A.H. 502 (= A.D. 1108–9).

[4] The readings vary. A. has محمّد ضخم ; B. محمّد حكيم ; L. ضخم only.

[5] A. adds "in the year [A.H.] 502."

fulfilling the utmost of my endeavour in this matter; but no improvement in his health took place. Three days elapsed. At the time of evening prayer I returned, thinking that the patient would pass away at midnight. I went up on to the roof, but could hardly sleep for anxiety. In the morning when I awoke I said to myself, 'The patient will have passed away.' I turned my face in that direction, but heard no sound [of lamentation] which might indicate his passing. I repeated the *Fátiḥa*, and hastened in that direction, saying: 'O my God and my Lord, Thou Thyself hast said in the Sure Book and Indubitable Scripture, "*And we send down in the Qur'án what is a Healing and a Mercy to true believers.*"'[1] For I was filled with regret, seeing that he was a young man, and in easy circumstances. Then I performed the minor ablution, went to the oratory, and repeated the customary prayer. One knocked at the door of the house. When I went to look who was there, it was one of his household, who gave good tidings, saying, 'He hath passed out of danger'; and, on my enquiring when, added, 'Just now he obtained relief.' Then I knew that the patient had been relieved by the blessing of the *Fátiḥa* of the Scripture, and that this draught had been dispensed from the Divine Dispensary. For I have put this to the proof, administering this draught in many cases, in all of which it proved beneficial, and resulted in restoration to health."

Therefore the physician should be of good faith, and should venerate the commands and prohibitions of the Holy Law. And on the science of Medicine he should read the "Aphorisms" (*Fuṣúl*) of Hippocrates, the "Questions" (*Masá'il*) of Ḥunayn b. Isḥáq,[2] the "Guide" (*Murshid*) of Muḥammad b. Zakariyyá of Ray (ar-Rázi),[3] and Nílí's "Commentary"[4]; and after he has read and learned these

[1] Qur'án, xvii, 84.

[2] See Wüstenfeld's *Geschichte d. Arab. Aerzte*, No. 69, pp. 26–29. He was born A.H. 194 (A.D. 800), and died A.H. 260 (A.D. 873).

[3] Ibid., No. 98, pp. 40–49. He is known in Europe as Rasis or Rhases.

[4] For شرح نبلی A. has شرح نیلی.

volumes above enumerated with a kind and careful master, he should diligently study with a congenial teacher the following intermediate works, to wit, the "Thesaurus" (*Dhakhíra*) of Thábit b. Qurra, the *Manṣúrí*[1] of Muḥammad b. Zakariyyá of Ray, the "Direction" (*Hidáya*) of the younger[2] Abú Bakr, or the "Sufficiency" (*Kifáya*) of Aḥmad Farrukh, or the "Aims" (*Aghráḍ*) of Sayyid Ismá'íl Jurjání.[3] Then he should take up one of the more detailed treatises, such as the "Sixteen (Treatises," *Sitta 'ashar*) of Galen, or the "Compendium" (*Ḥáwí*) of Muḥammad b. Zakariyyá, or the "Complete Practitioner" (*Kámilu'ṣ-Ṣaná'at*), or the "Hundred Chapters" (*Ṣad Báb*) of Abú Sahl Masíḥí,[4] or the *Qánún* of Abú 'Alí (Avicenna),[5] or the *Dhakhíra-i-Khwárazmsháhí*,[6] and read it in his leisure moments; or, if he desires to be independent of other works, he may content himself with the *Qánún*.

The Lord of the Two Worlds and the Guide of the Two Grosser Races says: "*Every kind of game is in the belly of the wild ass.*"[7] All this has been set forth by the *Qánún*, so that much may be effected therewith; and whoever has mastered the first volume of the *Qánún*, to him nothing will be hidden of the general principles and applications of Medicine, for if Hippocrates and Galen could return to life, it would be proper that they should do reverence to this book. Yet have I heard a wonderful thing, to wit, that one hath taken exception to Abú 'Alí in respect of this work,

[1] See Wüstenfeld, op. cit., p. 43, No. 2. The full title of the work is: 'كتاب الطبّ المنصوري.

[2] Or "later" (آخرين), but A. reads اخوين. I cannot identify this person.

[3] See Wüstenfeld, op cit., No. 165, p. 95.

[4] Avicenna's master, d. A.H. 390 (A.D. 1000). See Wüstenfeld, loc. cit., pp. 59, 60, No. 118.

[5] See n. 1 on p. 107 *supra*.

[6] See Rieu's *Persian Catalogue*, pp. 466, 467.

[7] Meaning that every kind of game is inferior to the wild ass. It is said proverbially of anyone who excels his fellows. See Lane's *Arabic Lexicon*, p. 2357, s.v. فرأ.

and hath embodied his objections in a book, which he hath named "the Rectification of the Qánún"[1]; and it is as though I looked at both books, and perceived what a distinguished man the author of the first was, while the author of the second merits only censure. For what right has anyone to find fault with so great a man, when the very first question which he meets with in a book of his which he comes across is difficult to his comprehension? For four thousand years the physicians of antiquity travailed in spirit and melted their very souls in order to reduce the science of Medicine to some fixed order, yet could not effect this, until, after the lapse of this period, that absolute philosopher and most mighty thinker Aristotle portioned and parcelled out[2] Logic and Philosophy as in a balance, and measured them by the measure of analogy, so that all doubt and ambiguity departed from them, and they were established on a sure and critical basis. And during those fifteen centuries which have elapsed since his time, no philosopher has won to the inmost essence of his doctrine, nor travelled the high road of his pre-eminence, save that most excellent of the moderns, the Philosopher of the East and the West, the Proof of Islám,[3] Abú 'Alí b. 'Abdu'lláh b. Síná (Avicenna). He who finds fault with these two great men will have cast himself out from the company of the wise, ranked himself with madmen, and proved himself to be of the number of those who lack intelligence. May God (blessed and exalted is He) keep us from such stumblings and vain imaginings!

So, if the physician hath mastered the first volume of the *Qánún*, and hath attained to forty years of age, he will be worthy of confidence; and when he hath reached this degree, he should keep ever with him some of the smaller treatises

[1] اصلاح قانون.

[2] L. has 'منطق و حکمت صُرّه و نقد کرد'. For صرّه و A. substitutes حدود. In the margin of L. صرّه is glossed as = جمع.

[3] A. has "the Proof of God unto His creatures."

composed by proved masters, such as the "Gift of Kings" (*Tuḥfatu'l-Mulúk*) of Muḥammad Zakariyyá [ar-Rází], or the *Kifáya* of Ibn Sandíno of Iṣfahán, or the "Provision against all sorts of error in Medical Treatment" (*Tadáruku anwá'i'l-khaṭá fi't-tadbíri'ṭ-ṭibbí*), of which Abú 'Alí (Avicenna) is the author; or the *Khafiyyu'l-'Alá'í*,[1] or the "Memoranda" (*Yádigár*) of Sayyid Isma'íl Jurjání.[2] For no reliance can be placed on the Memory, which is located in the posterior part of the brain, for it may delay to afford him assistance in carrying out these prescriptions.

Therefore every king who would choose a physician must see that these conditions which have been enumerated are found in him; for it is no light matter to commit one's life and soul into the hands of any ignorant quack, or to entrust the care of one's health to any reckless charlatan.

Anecdote xxxii.

Bukht-Yíshú',[3] a Christian of Baghdad, was a skilful physician and a true and tender man; and he was attached to the service of al-Ma'mún the Caliph. Now one of the children of Háshim, a kinsman of al-Ma'mún, was attacked with dysentery, and al-Ma'mún, being greatly attached to him, sent Bukht-Yíshú' to treat him. So he, for al-Ma'mún's sake, girded up his loins in service, and treated him in various ways, but to no purpose, for the case passed beyond his powers. So Bukht-Yíshú' was ashamed before al-Ma'mún; but al-Ma'mún said to him: "Be not ashamed, for thou didst fulfil thine utmost endeavour, but God Almighty doth not desire that it should succeed. Acquiesce in Fate, even as we have acquiesced." Bukht-Yíshú', seeing al-Ma'mún thus hopeless, replied: "One other remedy remains, and it is a perilous one; but, trusting to the fortune of the Prince of Believers, I will attempt it, and perchance God Most High may cause it to succeed."

[1] See Ḥájí Khalífa, No. 4,738.
[2] See Wüstenfeld, op. cit., p. 95, No. 166. He died A.H. 530.
[3] See Wüstenfeld, op. cit., p. 17, No. 30. Concerning this and similar names, see Noeldeke's *Geschichte d. Artakhshír-i-Pápakán*, p. 49, n. 4.

Now the patient was going to stool fifty or sixty times a day. So Bukht-Yishú' prepared a purgative and administered it to him; and on the day whereon he took the purgative, his diarrhœa was still further increased; but next day it stopped. So the physicians asked him, "What hazardous treatment was that which thou didst adopt yesterday?" He answered: "The *materies morbi* of this diarrhœa was from the brain, and until it was dislodged from the brain the flux would not cease. I feared that if I administered a purgative the patient's strength might not be equal to the increased diarrhœa; but at length, when I plucked up heart, [I saw that] there was hope in giving the purgative, but none in withholding it. So I gave it, and God Most High vouchsafed a cure; and my opinion was justified, namely, that if the purgative were withheld, only the death of the patient was to be expected; but that if it were administered, there was a possibility of either life or death. Therefore, seeing that to give the purgative was the better course, I administered it."

Anecdote xxxiii.

The great Shaykh Abú 'Alí Síná (Avicenna) relates as follows in the "Book of the Origin and the Return" (*Kitábu'l-Mabdá wa'l-Ma'ád*), at the end of the section on Contingent Being:—

"A curious anecdote hath come to me which I have heard related.[1] A certain physician presented himself at the court of one of the House of Sámán, and was well received, and rose to so high a position of trust that he used to enter the women's apartments and feel the pulses of its carefully-guarded and closely-veiled inmates.

[1] L. has درکتاب مبدأ و معاد در آخر فصل امکان وجود نادرهٔ عن هذه النفس همیگوید. A. after نادرهٔ adds بمن رسید که شنودم and reads . . که . . رسید و شنودم که.

One day he was sitting with the King in the women's apartments in a place where it was impossible for any [other] male creature to pass. The King demanded food, and it was brought by the handmaidens. One of these presided over the table. As she was placing it on the ground, she bent down.[1] When she desired to stand upright again, she was unable to do so, but remained as she was, by reason of a rheumatic swelling of the joints.[2] The King turned to the physician and said, 'Cure her at once in whatever way you can.' Here was no opportunity for any physical method of treatment, since for such no appliances were available. So the physician bethought himself of a psychical treatment, and bade them remove the veil from her head, whereon she made a movement. Then he bade them remove her skirt,[3] whereon she raised her head and stood upright.

"'What method of procedure was this?' enquired the King. 'At that juncture,' replied the physician, 'a rheumatic swelling appeared in her joints. I bade them uncover her head, that perchance she might be ashamed, and might make some movement because this condition was displeasing to her. So the whole of her head and face was uncovered, and anger was apparent therein.[4] I then abandoned this, and ordered her skirt to be removed. She was filled with shame, and a flush of heat was produced within her, such that it dissolved the rheumatic humour. Then she stood upright, and, restored to her erect position, became sound once again.'

"Had this physician not been skilled in his art, he would never have thought of this treatment; and had he failed,

[1] For L.'s reading . . خوان بر زمین نهاد دو تو شد . A. has.—
خوان از سر خوانگهش درو گرفت ' دو تو شد و بر زمین نهاد . .

[2] L. has ' بجهة ریح غلیظی که در مفاصل او حادث آمد.

[3] Literally "trousers," of the kind worn by women in the East.

[4] Instead of تغیّر پدید آمد (L.'s reading) A. has تغیّر نگرفت , "she underwent no change"

he would have forfeited the King's regard. Hence a knowledge of natural science[1] and an apprehension of its facts form a part of this subject."

Anecdote xxxiv.

Another of the House of Sámán, Amír Manṣúr b. Núḥ b. Naṣr,[2] became afflicted with an ailment which grew chronic, and remained established, and the physicians were unable to cure it. So the Amír Manṣúr sent messengers to summon Muḥammad b. Zakariyyá of Ray to treat him. Muḥammad b. Zakariyyá came as far as the Oxus, but when he saw it he said: "I will not embark in the boat: God Most High saith, '*Do not cast yourselves into peril with your own hands*'[3]; and, again, it is surely a thing remote from wisdom voluntarily to place one's self in so hazardous a position." Ere the Amír's messenger had gone to Bukhárá and returned, he had composed the treatise entitled *Manṣúrí*.[4] So when a notable arrived with a special led-horse, bringing a message intermingled with promises of reward, he handed this *Manṣúrí* to him, saying: "I am this book, and by this book thou canst attain thine object, so that there is no need of me."

When the book reached the Amír he was in grievous suffering, wherefore he sent a thousand dínárs and one of his own private horses, saying: "Strive to move him by all these kind attentions, but, if they prove fruitless, bind his hands and feet, place him in the boat, and fetch him across." So, just as the Amír had commanded, they urgently entreated Muḥammad b. Zakariyyá, but to no purpose. Then they bound his hands and feet, placed him in the boat, and, when they had ferried him across the river, released him. Then they brought the led-horse, fully caparisoned, before him, and he mounted in the best

[1] So L., which reads طبیعی, but A. has طبع, "human nature."

[2] That is, Manṣúr I. who reigned A.H. 350–366 (A.D. 961–976). This anecdote is given in the *Akhláq-i-Jalálí* (ed. Lucknow, A.H. 1283), pp. 168–170.

[3] Qur'án, ii, v. 191.

[4] See n. 1 on p. 110 *supra*.

of humours, and set out for Bukhárá. And when they enquired of him, saying, "We feared to bring thee across the water lest thou shouldst cherish enmity against us, but thou didst not so, nor do we see thee vexed in heart," he replied: "I know that every year several thousand persons cross the Oxus without being drowned, and that I too should probably not be drowned; still, it was possible that I might perish, and if this had happened they would have continued till the Resurrection to say, 'A foolish fellow was Muḥammad b. Zakariyyá, in that, of his own free will, he embarked in a boat and so was drowned.' But when they bound me, I escaped all danger of censure; for then they would say, 'They bound the poor fellow's hands and feet, so that he was drowned.' Thus should I have been excused, not blamed, in case of my being drowned."

When they reached Bukhárá, he saw the Amír and began to treat him, exerting his powers to the utmost, but without relief to the patient. One day he came in before the Amír and said: "To-morrow I am going to try another method of treatment, but for the carrying out of it you will have to sacrifice such-and-such a horse and such-and-such a mule," the two being both animals of note, so that in one night they had gone forty parasangs.

So next day he took the Amír to the hot bath of Jú-yi-Múlíyán, outside the palace, leaving that horse and mule ready equipped and tightly girt in the charge of his own servant; while of the King's retinue and attendants he suffered not one to enter the bath. Then he brought the King into the middle of the hot bath, and poured over him warm water, after which he prepared a draught and gave it to him to drink. And he kept him there till such time as the humours in his joints were matured.

Then he himself went out and put on his clothes, and, taking a knife in his hand, came in, and stood for a while reviling the King, saying: "Thou didst order me to be bound and cast into the boat, and didst conspire against my life. If I do not destroy thee as a punishment for this, I am not Muḥammad b. Zakariyyá!"

The Amír was furious, sprang from his place, and, partly from anger, partly from fear of the knife and dread of death, rose to his feet. When Muḥammad b Zakariyyá saw the Amír on his feet, he turned round and went out from the bath, and he and his servant mounted, the one the horse, the other the mule, and turned their faces towards the Oxus. At the time of the second prayer they crossed the river, and halted nowhere till they reached Merv. When Muḥammad b. Zakariyyá reached Merv, he alighted, and wrote a letter to the Amír, saying: "May the life of the King be prolonged in health of body and effective command! According to agreement this servant treated his master, doing all that was possible. There was, however, an extreme weakness in the natural caloric, and the treatment of the disease by ordinary means would have been a protracted affair. I therefore abandoned it, and carried you to the hot bath for psychical treatment, and administered a draught, and left you so long as to bring about a maturity of the humours. Then I angered the King, so that an increase in the natural caloric was produced, and it gained strength until those humours, already softened, were dissolved. But henceforth it is not expedient that a meeting should take place between myself and the King."

Now after the Amír had risen to his feet and Muḥammad b. Zakariyyá had gone out, the Amír sat down and at once fainted. When he came to himself he went forth from the bath and called to his servants, saying, "Where has the physician gone?" They answered, "He came out from the bath, and mounted the horse, while his attendant mounted the mule, and went off."

Then the Amír knew what object he had had in view. So he came forth on his own feet from the hot bath; and tidings of this ran through the city, and his servants and retainers and people rejoiced greatly, and gave alms, and offered sacrifices, and held high festival. But they could not find the physician, seek him as they might. And on the seventh day Muḥammad b. Zakariyyá's servant arrived, riding the horse and leading the mule, and presented the letter. The Amír read it, and was astonished, and excused him, and sent him a horse, and a robe of honour, and equipment, and a cloak, and arms, and a turban, and a male slave, and a handmaiden; and further commanded that there should be assigned to him in Ray from the estates of al-Ma'mún[1] a yearly allowance of two[2] thousand dínárs and two hundred ass-loads of corn. These marks of honour he forwarded to him by the hand of a trusty messenger, together with his apologies. So the Amír completely regained his health, and Muḥammad b. Zakariyyá attained his object.

Anecdote XXXV.

Ma'mún Khwárazmsháh[3] had an accomplished Minister named Abu'l-Ḥasan Aḥmad b. Muḥammad. He was a man of learning and a friend of scholars, and consequently many philosophers and men of erudition, such as Abú 'Alí b. Síná, Abú Sahl Masíḥí, Abu'l-Ḥasan Khammár, Abú Naṣr 'Arráq, and Abú Rayḥán [al-Bírúní],[4] gathered about his court.

Now Abú Naṣr 'Arráq was the nephew of Khwárazmsháh, and in all branches of the exact sciences he was second only to Ptolemy the Philosopher; while Abú 'Alí [b Síná] and Abú Sahl Masíḥí were the successors of Aristotle[5] in

[1] The text has از املاک مامون, but perhaps the last word is to be taken as meaning "settled," "tranquil."

[2] So in L., and so corrected in A. from "twelve thousand."

[3] See p. viii of the Preface to Sachau's translation of al-Bírúní's *Chronology of the Ancient Nations*, and the same scholar's article *Zur Geschichte und Chronologie von Chwârezm* in the *Sitzungsberichte d. Wiener Akademie* for 1863.

[4] The first, second, and last of these learned men have been already mentioned. The third is probably Abu'l-Khayr al-Ḥasan . . . Ibnu'l-Khammár (Wüstenfeld's *Geschichte d. Arab. Aerzte*, No. 115, pp. 58, 60), who died A.H. 381 (A.D. 991).

[5] The texts have "of Arisṭú and Arisṭáṭális," as though they were two different persons, instead of two forms of the same name.

the science of Philosophy, which includes all sciences; and Abu'l-Ḥasan Khammár was the third after Hippocrates and Galen in the science of Medicine. And all these were, in this their service, independent of worldly cares, and maintained with one another familiar intercourse and pleasant correspondence.

But Fortune, as is its custom, disapproved of this; though the King would not willingly have destroyed this happiness of theirs, or brought these pleasant days to an end. So a notable arrived from Sulṭán Maḥmúd Yamínu'd-Dawla with a letter, whereof the purport was as follows: "I have heard that there are in attendance on Khwárazmsháh several men of learning, each unrivalled in his science, such as So-and-so and So-and-so. You must send them to my court, so that they may attain the honour of attendance thereat. We rely on being enabled to profit by their knowledge and skill, and request this favour on the part of Khwárazmsháh."

Now the bearer of this message was Khwája Ḥusayn 'Alí Míká'íl, who was one of the most accomplished men of his age, and the wonder of his time amongst his contemporaries, while the prosperity of Sulṭán Yamínu'd-Dawla continued ever on the increase in the zenith of dominion and empire, and the kings of the time used to treat him with every respect and do him homage, and night and day lay down in fear of him. So Khwárazmsháh entertained Ḥusayn 'Alí Míká'íl in the best of lodgings, and ordered him to be supplied with all materials suitable for a prolonged stay; but, before according him an audience, he summoned the philosophers and laid before them the King's letter, saying: "The King is strong, and has a large army recruited from Khorásán and India; and he covets 'Iráq. I cannot refuse to obey his order, or be disobedient to his mandate. What say ye on this matter?"

They answered, "We cannot abandon thy service, nor will we in any wise go to him." But Abú Naṣr and Abu'l-Ḥasan and Abú Rayḥán were eager to go, having heard accounts of the King's munificent gifts and presents. Then said Khwárazmsháh, "I will summon you before me,[1] and do you take your own way." Then he equipped Abú 'Alí [b. Síná] and Abú Sahl, and arranged a plan for them, and sent with them a guide, and they set off through the desert towards Mázandarán.

Next day Khwárazmsháh accorded Ḥusayn 'Alí Míká'íl an audience, and heaped on him all sorts of compliments. "I have read the letter," said he, "and have acquainted myself with its contents and with the King's command. Abú 'Alí and Abú Sahl are gone, but I will provide equipment for Abú Naṣr and Abú Rayḥán and Abu'l-Ḥasan,[2] so that they may enjoy the honour of entering that August Presence." So in a little while he provided their outfit, and despatched them in the company of Khwája Ḥusayn Míká'íl to Balkh. So they came into the presence of Sulṭán Yamínu'd-Dawla, and joined the King's Court.

Now it was Abú 'Alí [b. Síná] whom the King chiefly desired. He commanded Abú Naṣr the painter to draw his portrait on paper, and he ordered the other artists to make forty copies of the portrait, and these he despatched in all directions, placing them in the hands of persons of note, to whom he said, "There is a man after this likeness, whom they call Abú 'Alí b. Síná. Seek him out and send him to me."

Now when Abú 'Alí and Abú Sahl departed from Khwárazmsháh,[3] ere morning came they had travelled fifteen parasangs. When it was morning they alighted at a place where there were wells, and Abú 'Alí took up an astrological table to see under what ascendant they had started on their journey. "We shall lose our way," said he, "and experience hardships." Said Abú Sahl: "We acquiesce in God's decree. Indeed, I know that I shall not come safely through this journey, for in these two days

[1] L.'s reading is: 'شمارا پیش خوانم. A. adds the words در ترک after شما.

[2] Here and elsewhere A. has *Ḥusayn* for *Ḥasan*.

[3] So A. L. has "Khwárazm."

the passage of the degree of my ascendant reaches Capricorn, and that is decisive,[1] so that no hope remains to me. Henceforth our intercourse of souls is at an end."[2]

Then a wind arose and clouds gathered. Abú 'Alí relates as follows. On the fourth day a dust-storm arose, and the world was darkened. They lost their way, for the wind had obliterated the tracks. When the wind lulled, their guide was a thousand times more astray than before; no water was obtainable; and, by reason of the heat of the desert of Khwárazm, Abú Sahl Masíḥí passed away to the World of Eternity. The guide turned back, while Abú 'Alí, with a thousand hardships and difficulties, reached Abíwurd, whence he went to Ṭús, and finally happened on Níshápúr.

There he found a number of persons who were seeking for Abú 'Alí. He alighted in a quiet spot, where he abode several days, and thence he turned his face towards Gurgán. Qábús,[3] who was king of that province, was a great and accomplished man, and a friend to men of learning. Abú 'Alí knew that there no harm would befal him. When he reached Gurgán, he alighted at a caravanseray. One day a person fell sick in his neighbourhood. Abú 'Alí treated him, and he got better. It is related that Abú 'Alí continued to live in Gurgán,[4] and that his income became considerable and went on increasing day by day. Some time elapsed thus, until one of the relatives of Qábús fell sick. The physicians set themselves to treat him, striving and exerting themselves to the utmost, but the disease was not cured. Now Qábús was greatly attached

[1] The text has که تسییر درجهٔ طالع من درین دو روز بعیّوق مرسد وآن [A. واو] قاطع است. The term *tasyír* is explained at p. 230 of Van Vloten's ed. of the *Mafátíḥu'l-'ulúm*.

[2] This last sentence is in A. only.

[3] Qábús b. Washmgír Shamsu'l-Ma'álí, reigned A.H. 366–371 and again A.H. 388–403. To him al-Bírúní dedicated his *Chronology of Ancient Nations*. See Sachau's English translation of that work, Preface, p. viii.

[4] For L.'s reading در گرگان بزیست A. has همی نگریست.

to him. So one of the servants of Qábús did obeisance before him and said: "Into such-and-such a caravanserai hath entered a young man who is a physician, and whose efforts are singularly blessed, so that several persons have been cured at his hands." So Qábús bade them seek him out and bring him to the patient.

So they sought out Abú 'Alí and brought him to the sick man. He saw a youth of comely countenance, whereon the hair had scarcely begun to show itself, and of symmetrical proportions. He sat down, felt his pulse, asked to see his urine, inspected it, and said, "I want a man who knows all the districts and the quarters of this province." So they brought one; and Abú 'Alí placed his hand on the patient's pulse, and bade the other mention the names of the different quarters and districts of Gurgán. So the man began, and continued until he reached the name of a quarter at the mention of which, as he uttered it, the patient's pulse gave a strange flutter. Then Abú 'Alí said, "Now I must have someone who knows all the streets in this quarter." They brought such an one. "Repeat," said Abú 'Alí, "the names of all the houses in this district." So he repeated them till he reached the name of a house at the mention of which the patient's pulse gave the same flutter. "Now," said Abú 'Alí, "I want someone who knows all the households." They brought such an one, and he began to repeat them until he reached a name at the mention of which that same strange flutter was apparent.

Then said Abú 'Alí, "It is finished." Thereupon he turned to the confidential advisers of Qábús, and said: "This lad is in love with such-and-such a girl, in such-and-such a house, in such-and-such a street, in such-and-such a quarter: the girl's face is the patient's cure." The patient, who was listening, heard what was said, and in shame hid his face beneath the clothes. When they made enquiries, it was even as Abú 'Alí had said.[1] Then they

[1] Compare the precisely similar narrative in the first story of the first book of the *Mathnawí* of Jalálu'd-Dín Rúmí, and also a passage in the section of the *Dhakhíra-i-Khwárazmsháhí* (Book vi, Guftár i, Juz' 2, ch. 3), of which this

reported this matter to Qábús, who was amazed thereat and said, "Bring him before me." So Abú 'Alí b. Síná was brought before Qábús.

Now Qábús had a copy of Abú 'Alí's portrait, which Yamínu'd-Dawla had sent to him. "Why, here is Abú 'Alí!" exclaimed he. "Yes, O most puissant Prince," replied the other. Then Qábús came down from his throne, advanced several paces to meet Abú 'Alí, embraced him, conversed genially with him, sat down beside him, and said, "O greatest and most accomplished philosopher of the world, explain to me the rationale of this treatment!" "O Sire," answered Abú 'Alí, "when I inspected his pulse and urine, I became convinced that his complaint was love, and that he had fallen thus sick through keeping his secret. Had I enquired of him, he would not have told me; so I placed my hand on his pulse while they repeated in succession the names of the different quarters, and when it came to the name of the quarter of his beloved, love moved him, and his heart was stirred, so that I knew she was a dweller in that quarter. Then I enquired the streets, and when I reached the street in question that same movement occurred, and I knew that she dwelt in that street. Then I enquired the names of the households in that street, and the same phenomenon occurred when the house of his beloved was named, so that I knew the house also. Then they made mention of the names of its inhabitants, and when he heard the name of his beloved, he was greatly affected, so that I knew the name of his sweetheart also. Then I told him my conclusion, and he could not deny it, but was compelled to confess the truth."

is a translation:—"Now the lover's pulse is variable and irregular, especially when he sees the object of his affections, or hears her name, or gets tidings of her. In this way one can discover, in the case of one who conceals his love and the name of his beloved, who is the object of his passion, and that in the following way. The physician should place his finger on the patient's pulse, and unexpectedly order the names of those persons amongst whom it may be surmised that his sweetheart is to be found to be repeated, whereupon it will appear from the patient's behaviour who his beloved is and what her name is. Avicenna (upon whom be God's Mercy) says: 'I have tried this plan, and have succeeded by it in finding out who the beloved object was.'"

Qábús was greatly astonished, and indeed there was good reason for astonishment. "O most eminent and most excellent philosopher of the world," said he, "both the lover and the beloved are the children of my sisters, and are cousins to one another. Choose, then, an auspicious moment that I may unite them in marriage." So the Master [Avicenna] chose a fortunate hour, and in it they were united, and that prince was cured of the ailment which had brought him to death's door. And thereafter Qábús maintained Abú 'Alí in the best manner possible, and thence he went to Ray, and finally became minister to 'Alá'u'd-Dawla, as is well known in history.

Anecdote xxxvi.

The author of the *Kámilu'ṣ-Ṣaná'at*[1] was physician to 'Aḍudu'd-Dawla[2] in Párs, in the city of Shíráz. Now in that city there was a porter who used to carry loads of four hundred and five hundred maunds on his back. And every five or six months he would be attacked by headache, and become restless, remaining so for ten[3] days and nights. One time he was attacked by headache, and when seven or eight days had elapsed, he several times determined to destroy himself. At length one day this physician passed by the door of his house. The porter's brother ran to meet him, did reverence to him, and, conjuring him by God Most High, told him his brother's condition. "Bring him to me," said the physician. So they called him before the physician, who saw that he was a big man, of bulky frame, wearing on his feet a pair of shoes each of which weighed a maund and a half. Then the physician asked for and examined his urine; after which, "Bring him with me into the open country," said

[1] See Brockelmann's *Gesch. d. Arab. Litt.*, p. 237, No. 10. His name was 'Alí b. al-'Abbás al-Majúsí, and he died A.H. 384 (A.D. 994).

[2] The second prince of the House of Buwayh, reigned A.H. 338–372 (A.D. 949–982).

[3] So A., but L. has "two."

he. They did so. On their arrival there, he bade his servant take the turban from his head, and cast it round his neck. Then he ordered another servant to take the shoes off the porter's feet and kick him on the back of the neck. The porter's sons wept, but the physician was a man of consideration, so that they could say nothing. Then the physician ordered his servant to throw the turban round his neck, to mount his horse, and to make the porter run round the plain. The servant did as he was bid. Blood began to flow from the porter's nostrils. "Now," said the physician, "let him alone, that the blood may flow from him, for he stinketh worse than a corpse." The man fell asleep amidst the blood which flowed from his nose, and three hundred dirhams' weight of blood escaped from his nostrils. They bore him thence, and he slept for a day and a night, and his headache passed away and never again returned.

Then 'Aḍudu'd-Dawla questioned the physician as to the rationale of this treatment. "O King," he replied, "for some while the blood had coagulated[1] in his head, and it was impossible to relieve this congestion by means of belladonna,[2] so I devised another treatment, which proved successful."

Anecdote xxxvii.

Melancholia is a disease which physicians often fail to treat successfully, for, though all melancholic diseases are chronic, melancholia is a pathological condition which is [especially] slow to pass.

[1] Perhaps "coagulated" is too strong a word for افسرده, and we should rather translate "for some while he had suffered from congestion of the head" or "cerebral congestion."

[2] 'نقبرا [A., B. نا بارج [يارج. The word بارج, explained as = سگ انگور or عنب الثعلب, seems to mean belladonna. The word نقبرا I do not understand.

Abu'l-Ḥasan b. Yaḥyá, in his work entitled the "Hippocratic Therapeutics" (*Mu'álaja-i-Buqráṭí*),[1] a book the like of which hath been composed by no one on the Art of Medicine, hath reckoned up the leaders of thought, sages, physicians, scholars, and philosophers who have been afflicted by this disease, for there were many of them; and he continues thus:—

"My master Abú Ja'far b. Muḥammad Abú Sa'd[2] al-Nashawí, commonly known as Ṣarakh,[3] related to me," says he, "on the authority of the Imám Shaykh Muḥammad b. al-'Aqíl al-Qazwíní, on the authority of the Amír Fakhru'd-Dawla Kálinjár the Buwayhid, that one of the princes of the House of Buwayh was attacked by melancholy, and was in such wise affected by the disease that he imagined himself to have been transformed into a cow. Every day he would low like a cow, causing annoyance to everyone, and saying, 'Kill me, so that a good stew may be prepared from my flesh'; until matters reached such a pass that he would eat nothing, and the physicians were unable to do him any good.

"Now at this juncture Abú 'Alí (Avicenna) was prime minister, and the king 'Alá'u'd-Dawla Muḥammad b. Washmgír had the fullest confidence in him, and had entrusted into his hands all the affairs of the kingdom, and placed under his judgment and discretion all matters. And, indeed, since Alexander the Great, whose minister was Aristotle, no king had such a minister as Abú 'Alí. And during the time that he was minister, he used to rise up every morning before dawn and write a couple of pages of the *Shifá*.[4] Then, when the true dawn appeared, he

[1] See Brockelmann's *Gesch. d. Arab. Litt.*, p. 237, where his name is given as Abu'l-Ḥasan 'Alí b. Muḥammad aṭ-Ṭabarí. He was court physician to the Buwayhid prince Ruknu'd-Dawla about A.H. 360 (A.D. 970). MSS. of the work cited exist at Oxford, Munich, and in the India Office.

[2] A has Sa'dí.

[3] So all texts, صرخ.

[4] One of Avicenna's most celebrated works. See the *British Museum Arabic Catalogue*, p. 746a, and the *Supplement* to the same, No. 711, pp. 484, 486.

used to give audience to his disciples, such as Kiyá Ra'ís Bahmanyár, Abú Mansúr Zila,[1] 'Abdu'l-Wáhid Jurjání, Sulayman of Damascus, and me, Abú Kálinjár. We used to continue our studies till the morning grew bright, and then perform our prayers behind him; and as soon as he came forth he was met at the gate of his house by a thousand mounted men, comprising the dignitaries and notables, as well as such as had boons to crave, or were in difficulties. Then the minister would mount, and this company would attend him to the Government Offices. By the time he arrived there, the number of horsemen had reached two thousand. And there he would remain until the morning prayer, and when he retired for refreshment all that company ate with him. Then he took his midday siesta, and when he rose up from this he would perform his prayer, wait on the King, and remain talking and conversing with him until the next prayer; and in all matters of importance there was no third person between him and the King.

"Our object in narrating these details is to show that the minister had no leisure time. Now when the physicians proved unable to cure this young man, the King's intercession was sought, so that he might bid his minister take the case in hand. So 'Alá'u'd-Dawla spoke to him to this effect, and he consented. Then said he, 'Good tidings to the patient, for the butcher has come to kill him!' When the patient heard this, he rejoiced. Then the minister mounted his horse, and came with his retinue to the gate of the patient's house. Taking a knife in his hand, he entered with two attendants, saying, 'Where is this cow, that I may kill it?' The patient made a noise like a cow, meaning, 'He is here.' The minister bade them bind him hand and foot in the middle of the house. The patient ran forward into the middle of the house and lay down on his right side, and they bound his hands and feet firmly, and 'Abú 'Alí then came forward, rubbing

[1] زیله.

the knives together, sat down, and placed his hand on his side, as is the custom of butchers. 'He is very lean,' said he, 'and not fit to be killed: he must eat fodder until he gets fat.' Then he rose up and came out, having bidden them loose his hands and feet, and place food before him, saying, 'Eat, so that thou mayst grow fat.' They did so, and he ate, and recovered his appetite, after which they administered to him drugs and draughts. 'This cow,' said Abú 'Alí, 'must be well fattened'; so the patient ate in the hope that he might grow fat and they might kill him; while the physicians applied themselves vigorously to treating him as the minister had indicated, and in a month's time he completely recovered."

All wise men will perceive that one cannot heal by such methods of treatment save by virtue of extreme excellence, perfect science, and unerring acumen.

Anecdote xxxviii.

In the reign of Maliksháh, and during part of the reign of Sulṭán Sanjar, there was at Herát a philosopher named Adíb Isma'íl, a very great and perfect man, who, however, derived his income from his receipts as a physician. By him many rare cures of this class were wrought.

One day he was passing through the sheep-slayers' market. A butcher was skinning a sheep, and was eating the warm fat which he took from its belly.[1] Khwája Isma'íl said to a grocer opposite him, "If at any time this fellow should die, inform me of it before they lay him in his grave." "Willingly," replied the grocer. When five or six months had elapsed, one morning it was rumoured abroad that such-and-such a butcher had died suddenly without any premonitory illness. The grocer also went to offer his condolences. He found a number of people tearing their garments, while others were consumed with grief, for

[1] So in L. A. has: "And every now and then he would put his hand into the sheep's belly, pull out some of the warm fat, and swallow it."

the dead man was young, and had little children. Then he remembered the words of Khwája Isma'íl, and hastened to bear the intelligence to him. Said the Khwája, "He has been a long time in dying." Then he arose, took his staff, went to the dead man's house, raised the sheet from the face of the corpse, and began to apply the remedies for apoplexy.[1] On the third day the dead man arose, and, though he remained paralytic, he lived for many years, and men were astonished, for that great man had seen from the first that he would be stricken by apoplexy.

Anecdote xxxix.

The Shaykhu'l-Islám 'Abdu'lláh Anṣárí (may God sanctify his spirit!) conceived a fanatical hatred of the above-mentioned man of science, and several times attempted to do him an injury, and burned his books. Now this fanatical dislike arose from religious motives, for the people of Herát believed that he could restore the dead to life, and this belief was injurious to his own pretensions.[2]

Now the Shaykh fell ill, and in the course of his illness the death-rattle become apparent. However much the physicians treated him, it availed nothing. They were in despair, and so sent a sample of his urine to the Khwája under the name of another, and requested him to prescribe. When he had inspected it, he said: "This is the urine of so-and-so, in whom the death-rattle has become apparent, and whom they are unable to treat. Bid them pound together a *sír* of pistachio-skins and a *sír*[3] of the sugar called *'askarí* and give it to him, so that he may recover; and give him this message: 'You should study science, and not burn men's books.'"

[1] سکته.

[2] So B. and L. (دعوی را), but A. reads عوامّ را, "was injurious to the common folk."

[3] For یک سر A. has یک سیه twice, and adds مغز after پوست.

So they made a confection of those two ingredients, and the patient ate it, and immediately the death-rattle ceased, and he recovered.

Anecdote xl.

In the time of Galen, one of the notables of Alexandria was attacked by pain in the finger-tips, and suffered great restlessness, being debarred from all repose. They informed Galen, who prescribed an unguent to be applied to his shoulders. As soon as they did this he was cured. Then they questioned Galen, saying, "What was [the rationale of] this treatment which thou didst adopt?" He replied: "This, that the source of a pain which attacks the finger-tips is the shoulder. I treated the root so that the branch might be cured."

Anecdote xli.

In the year A.H. 547 (= A.D. 1152–3),[1] when a battle took place at Durúward[2] between the King of the World Sanjar b. Maliksháh and my master 'Alá'u'd-Dawla al-Ḥusayn (may God immortalize their reigns!), and the Ghúrid army was so grievously smitten by the evil eye,[3] and I wandered about Herát in hiding, because I was connected with the House of Ghúr, and their enemies uttered all manner of accusations against them, and rejoiced malignantly over their reverse; in the midst of this state of things, I say, I chanced one night to be in the house of a certain noble man. When he had eaten bread, I went out to satisfy a need. That noble man, by reason of whom I came to be there, was praising me, saying: "Men know him as a poet, but, apart from his skill in poetry, he is a man

[1] L. has "447," both in figures and writing, an evident error, since Sanjar reigned A.H. 511–552, and 'Alá'u'd-Dín Husayn "Jahán-súz" A.H. 544–556. A. omits the figures, and only has "in the year forty-seven."

[2] See B. de Meynard's *Dict. de la Perse*, p. 228, but this reading is conjectural. L. has بدراویه, A. بدراوبه.

[3] لشکر غوررا چنان چشم زخمی افتاد.

of great attainments, well skilled in astrology, medicine, polite letter-writing, and other accomplishments."

When I returned to the company, the master of the house showed me much respect, as do those who are in need of some favour, and sat by me for a while. "O so-and-so," said he, "I have one only daughter, and, save her, no other near relative, and she is my treasure. Lately she has fallen a victim to a malady such that during the days of her monthly courses ten or fifteen *sirs*[1] of sanguineous matter come from her, and she is greatly weakened. We have consulted the physicians, several of whom have treated her, but it has availed nothing, for if this issue be stopped, she is attacked with pain and swelling in the stomach, and if it be renewed, it is increased in amount,[2] and she is much weakened, so that I fear its cessation, lest her strength should wholly decline." "Send me word," said I, "when next this state occurs."

When ten days had passed, the patient's mother came to fetch me, and brought her daughter to me. I saw a girl very comely, but despairing of life, and stricken with terror. She at once fell at my feet, saying: "O my father! For God's sake help me, for I am young, and have not yet seen the world." The tears sprang to my eyes, and I said, "Be of good cheer, this is an easy matter." Then I placed my fingers on her pulse. I found the artery strong, and her colour and complexion normal. It was at this time the season of summer, and most of the conditions of an enjoyable life[3] were present, such as a robust habit of body, a strong constitution, a healthy complexion, age, season, country,[4] and occupation. Then I summoned a phlebotomist

[1] A. has "maunds."

[2] L. has: . . و اگر باز شود زیات میرود. A. has:
و اگر می کشایند سیلان می افتد . .

[3] L. امور عشرت, A. امور عشرة.

[4] For L.'s reading, و بلد, A. has:
و هوای بلد (بلد ?) و عادت و اعراض مذیمه '

and bade him open the basilic vein in both her arms; and I sent away all the women. The bad blood continued to flow, and, by pressure and manipulation, I took from her a thousand dirhams' weight of blood, so that she fell down in a swoon. Then I bade them bring fire, and prepare roasted meat beside her, until the house was filled with the smoke of the roasting meat, and it entered her nostrils. Then she came to her senses, moved, groaned, and asked for a drink. Then I prepared for her a gentle stimulant, and treated her for a week, and she recovered, and that illness passed away, and her monthly courses resumed their normal condition. And I called her my daughter, and to-day she is to me as my other children.

Conclusion.

My object in writing this treatise and in setting forth this discourse is not to make mention of my merits or to show forth my services, but rather to guide the beginner, and to glorify my Lord, the learned and just King, Ḥusámu'd-Dowla wa'd-Dín, Helper of Islám and the Muslims, Pride of monarchs and kings, noblest of mankind, Shamsu'l-Ma'álí, Maliku'l-Umará, Abu'l-Ḥasan 'Alí b. Mas'úd b. al-Ḥusayn, Nuṣratu Amíri'l-Mú'minín (may God perpetuate his glory!), by whose high station the Kingly Office is magnified. May God (blessed and glorious is He!) continue to embellish it by his Beauty, and may the Divine Protection and Heavenly Grace be a buckler over the form and stature of both, and may the heart of my Lord and Benefactor Fakhru'd-Dawla wa'd-Dín, Bahá'u'l-Islám wa'l-Muslimín, King of the kings of the mountains, be rejoiced, not for a while but for ever, by the continuance of both!

Concluding Note by the Editor of the Ṭihrán ed. of A.H. 1305 (= A.D. 1887–8).

In the beneficent reign of the Sovereign Lord[1] of the nations, the King of kings who is like unto Alexander in pomp, the Remembrancer of Kisrá and Jamshíd, the Monarch of monarchs, the Shadow of God in the lands, by the regards of whose weighty mind all the sciences and arts enjoy the fullest ascendency, and the votaries of every sort of craft and cunning possess the most brilliant position, the King, son of a king and grandson of a king, and the Prince, son of a prince and grandson of a prince, SHÁH NÁṢIRU'D-DÍN QÁJÁR (may God prolong his Power, and extend his Life and his Reign!)—

> "*O King, who resemblest the Angels in exaltation,*
> *Whose name is held in fair renown by the Supreme Host!*"

By the auspicious traits of his nature the treatises of men of culture, which had been clothed in the raiment of oblivion, have become adorned with the ornament of print, while the dust of desolation has been removed from the senses of men of learning. Amongst such treatises is this *Chahár Maqála* of 'Arúḍí, whereof, until this time, the virgin sentences were hidden behind the curtain of concealment, and the maiden anecdotes lay latent and unknown in the leaves. This servant of the Heaven-high Court and house-bred slave of this Immortal Dynasty, Muḥammad Báqir Khán, son of the late Ḥájí Muḥammad Báqir Khán, Begler-begí, the Qájár, who has devoted most of his time to the transcription of written pages, undertook, at the desire of his High Reverence Mullá 'Alí Khwánsárí, to transcribe this also. Two manuscripts were examined, of which the one had been copied from the other. In the one there were bad mistakes, and in the other worse. It was as though a heap of gold had been acquired, but filled

[1] Literally "Master of the necks"

with alloy and dross. Thus, amongst other errors, تَمَم was written طميم, and حماحم ,حميم. Therefore, to the utmost of my power, I applied myself, while transcribing the book, to correcting as far as possible the words and sentences occurring in it. My prayer of my spiritual friends, who are the changers of the coins of ideas, is that if a chance mistake occur, or an erroneous idea or word appear, they will overlook it with gracious eyes, and will endeavour to read such correction into the text.

At the time of concluding, a chronogram expressing the date [of publication] occurred to me, and is here submitted:[1]

كتاب چهار مقاله کلاً صحیح در طبع آمد ' ١٣٠٥

By the desire of Ákhúnd-i-Mullá 'Alí Khwánsárí, A.H. 1305, and by the care of His Reverence Abu'l-Qásim, the noble heir of Ákhúnd-i-Mullá Muḥammad.

[1] The meaning is: "The Book of the *Four Discourses* hath been correctly printed in its entirety." The numerical values of the letters composing this sentence, when added up, give 1305.

INDEX OF PERSONS, PLACES, AND BOOKS.

PRINTED BY STEPHEN AUSTIN AND SONS, HERTFORD.

www.ingramcontent.com/pod-product-compliance
Lightning Source LLC
Chambersburg PA
CBHW030906050726
47500CB00009B/1120
* 9 7 8 3 3 3 7 3 8 4 7 3 9 *